Also By Steven Becker

Kurt Hunter Mysteries
Backwater Bay
Backwater Channel
Backwater Cove
Backwater Key
Backwater Pass
Backwater Tide

Mac Travis Adventures
Wood's Relic
Wood's Reef
Wood's Wall
Wood's Wreck
Wood's Harbor
Wood's Reach
Wood's Revenge
Wood's Betrayal

Tides of Fortune
Pirate
The Wreck of the Ten Sail
Haitian Gold

Will Service Adventure Thrillers
Bonefish Blues
Tuna Tango
Dorado Duet

Storm Series
Storm Rising
Storm Force

ISBN: 9781719966207

A KURT HUNTER MYSTERY

BACKWATER TIDE

LARGE
PRINT

STEVEN
BECKER

Dolores West

Chapter 1

Nervous didn't begin to describe how I felt as I released the tie-downs holding the pair of boards on the rack of Justine's car. Looking around the half-full parking lot of Bill Baggs State Park only made things worse. Men and women, attempting to identify their competition, took measured glances as they unloaded their equipment. Many people knew each other and though they were familiar with their respective abilities, they kept a careful eye out for new equipment as they greeted each other.

"Dad, I'm going with Justine to the registration tent. They're supposed to have some cool swag," Allie said.

Not wanting my daughter to see how nervous I was, I was glad she went as I took the top board off.

A stiff breeze, another addition to my pre-race nerves, tried to wrestle the twelve-and-a-half-foot standup paddleboard from my grasp. I was finally able to point the nose into the wind, allowing me to set it on the lee side of the car.

The next board, my new one, was a foot and a half longer at fourteen feet. Knowing what to expect now, I angled it properly before removing it and laying it against Justine's board. Now, if I could only know what to expect from the race, I could relax.

After taking the paddles, leashes, and PFDs from the back of the car, I leaned against the hood to wait for Justine and Allie. I found myself trying to guess the ages of the men as they walked by. Unfortunately I was one year shy of racing in the masters division and my peers were all younger. At thirty-nine, I was a virgin to standup paddleboard racing.

Justine, a much more experienced racer, had been my coach for the last few months. She had wanted me to set a goal for my first race. I knew better than to put the podium on the list and had decided a mid-pack finish would be acceptable. Now, remembering her advice about hydration, I leaned into the car and pulled out one of the water bottles filled with electrolytes. I had just finished it when I saw Justine and Allie coming toward me.

Watching the duo approach made me smile and helped calm my jitters. Justine had our race bibs and timing chips in hand; Allie was loaded with t-shirts, water bottles, and stickers.

"You ready for this?" Justine asked, handing me a velcro band with a timing chip attached.

I nodded and as I wrapped the strap around my ankle, I felt my anxiety rise again—this time about the finish. We had practiced beach starts and finishes; ditching the board at the end of the race and running through the finish line, where a sensor would record my time from the chip in the strap on my ankle, worried me. Often, after a hard paddle, I would stumble and sometimes fall before I got my land legs. There was also the matter of removing the leash. It sounded simple: just pull the velcro strap connecting me to the board off before hopping into the surf, but I had forgotten more than once, and that was just during training. I could see myself losing several places as I fell on the way to the finish line.

Cars and trucks were streaming into the near-full lot now and I waited while Justine drained a water bottle. "Should we go warm up?"

"Better do something. You look like you're gonna throw up," she said.

"I'm proud of you no matter what, Dad," Allie said.

Allie grabbed the paddles, leashes, PFDs, and two more water bottles. Justine and I each grabbed our boards and followed her to the beach. We stepped onto a wooden bridge that wove through a few sand dunes that had concealed the view of the ocean from the parking lot. After taking a few steps, my worst fear came to fruition. Standing on the tip of the peninsula known as Cape Florida, I now had an unobstructed view of the bay and ocean. The usually calm bay waters were rippled with wind waves; the ocean looked worse. The waves weren't that big by boating standards—maybe two to three feet—but to someone maneuvering on a fourteen-foot board built to the scale of a toothpick they looked intimidating.

It was the cross chop that really concerned me. I had gotten comfortable heading into the waves and running downwind, but my balance was not so good when the waves came from the side. For at least a mile of the four-mile short course we had decided was a good start for me, the wind would be on my side. I mentally reviewed the map of the course I'd etched into my brain—not that it needed to be, as I was sure to be following the pack.

"Everyone else has the same conditions," Justine said, reading my mind.

"Sure." I couldn't take my eyes off the water.

"Better get you wet," she said.

We reached an open area by the finish line and set up camp. An announcement warned that there would be a mandatory pre-race meeting in fifteen minutes. I could only hope it was going to be a course change.

"Come on," Justine said. With her inflatable PFD around her waist, she grabbed her paddle, and with the same hand lifted the board and headed to the water.

I looked at Allie, who gave me her best reassuring nod, and followed Justine into the surf. Even after a year and a half here I still braced myself, expecting the bite of the cold Pacific. Growing up in Northern California, with it's sixty-degree water, it had become a conditioned response for me to flinch whenever I first touched it. Even though I knew it was different here, I smiled for the first time when I felt the comforting eighty-degree temperature of Biscayne Bay.

"Kurt, get wet and warm up!" Justine called.

She was already past the small soupy shore break. I had gotten a lot of advice from her as we had trained together, and I'd snuck some off the internet as well. Getting wet was big, and I lay the board flat on the water and started through the waves to deeper water. When it reached chest deep, I ducked my head under before mounting the board. One of my fears immediately dissipated as I went to my knees. If you started out dry, a part of your brain wanted to stay that way. Getting wet right off the bat lessened my worries about falling.

That was a good thing because just as I started to stand a larger wave caught me by surprise and swept me off the board.

"You know how to brace," Justine called out as she effortlessly walked to the back of her board and spun it one hundred eighty degrees. "Come on. Let's do some sprints."

Hydrate, get wet, and sprint was her warmup

strategy. It had seemed counterintuitive at first to do a series of all-out sprints before a race, but we had done this in practice and as with her other advice it worked. The PA system blared another announcement that was lost on the wind, and I glanced down at my wrist to see if the fifteen minutes had elapsed. My watch was gone by design, however, another Justine recommendation. She blasted by me on her way to the beach and I followed. We left our boards above the water line and headed to the meeting.

My heart leapt when it was announced that the course had been changed. I could see from looking around that I wasn't the only one relieved. After a short safety briefing we were given ten minutes to get to the start line. Now that the clock was ticking, my brain had an immediate goal and it stopped the *you're going to fail* messages it had been sending since last night. Following Justine, I took another drink, grabbed our paddles and boards, and headed for the water. The second time out was much easier and I found myself in a group of paddlers, who I thought might be on my level, working their way to the start. Justine and I had decided to separate at this point. She was with the other top-tier racers doing the eight-mile course. The last thing I needed was her worrying about me. I glanced over and watched the nearby paddlers moving back and forth, trying to scope out the best line to start the race.

Then the horn blared, catching me off guard, and I had to catch myself and remember my plan. *Paddle your plan* had also been beaten into my head and I paused for a few seconds and let the frontrunners go before starting out at a moderate pace. Justine had warned me not to worry about the start. The elite racers and a large group of wannabes would go out fast. The water behind them would be churned up and hard to paddle. Staying clear of the pack turned out to be good advice as I watched bodies tumbling off their boards taking out the paddlers behind them as they went down. I breathed and smiled as I pushed by them. Justine had assured me that if I stayed with the plan I would pass the wannabes that went out too fast. Four miles would take close to an hour at my level so I had time and restrained myself, trying not to worry that I was in the back of the pack.

Justine was nowhere in sight as we rounded the point of Cape Florida. It was here that the course had changed and instead of the cross-chop I had feared, the calm water was only disturbed by the wakes of the boards in front of me. Originally the course had been designed to make a turn to the open Atlantic here, but because of the conditions the race organizers had changed it to go into the protected bay. We were getting close to the halfway mark and I was feeling strong, passing some of the wannabes as Justine had predicted. I was in the middle of the pack and moving up quickly. With each stroke I could feel my paddle grab water and propel me forward. I was close to the elusive zone.

Once past the point we left the protected water, and I felt the wind now that we were on the ocean side of the island. Stiltsville, a water-bound community of ramshackle buildings, lay ahead. The seven houses were at the northern extreme of Biscayne National Park, where I was based as a special agent. What was left of the original thirty structures, famous for their past guests (including presidents), then their being popularized by TV shows and movies, was the bane of the park. Nothing good happened here.

I turned my focus to the piling that jutted out of the water a quarter-mile ahead, which marked the turn back to the finish line. Instead of focusing on my approach and technique to make the hundred-eighty-degree turn, however, my attention turned to a boat that appeared to be brushing against the twelve-foot-high tower there. Several jet skis and chase boats were assigned to the race, but this didn't appear to be one of them.

The leaders worked their way around the marker, ignoring the boat, intent on the finish. The group I was in tightened as the racers prepared for the turn and I slid behind another board, using the wake to draft to an outside position. The angle was critical and when I reached forty-five degrees to the marker I started to stroke hard on my right, then cross over to my left and use the paddle as a rudder.

The board reacted and I passed several people before something in my brain changed gears. Even from here I could smell something was wrong, and I pulled off to the side and coasted to a stop at the stern of the boat. Maybe the single-minded intensity that had overcome me until now had allowed the other racers to miss it, but I had been around dead bodies before, and the second we turned upwind, I could tell there was one aboard the boat.

Chapter 2

The twelve-foot-tall lighted tower marked the beginning of the shoals surrounding Biscayne Channel as well as the northernmost point of the park. The drifting boat was just to the south, placing it inside the boundary. That made it my business. As my board slammed against the starboard side of the abandoned boat, I looked back at the racers rounding the tower. Several whom I had passed were turning the corner, ready to head for the finish. A strange feeling passed through me, a strange remorse, that felt like I had quit and let myself down. In response, I told myself I had been doing well and found whatever groove I had. Ignoring the drifting boat was not an option. I took one last look at the racers and turned my attention to the boat.

With one hand on a cleat, I reached my other down to my ankle and unfastened the velcro tab of the leash connecting me to the board. Keeping it in hand, I slipped the end under the cleat and secured it, attaching the board to the boat.

About forty feet overall and from the look of her a converted sportfisher, the boat was clearly a work vessel now. There was no tall superstructure common to these kinds of vessels, just a flybridge covered by a blue Bimini top. Two large winches were affixed to the rear deck. One, set slightly forward on the starboard side, had a small boom that was secured to a fitting on the gunwale. The other was set closer to the transom. Its cable ran to two huge pipes bent at ninety-degree angles. Called mailboxes or blowers, they were used by salvors to channel the force of the propellers to the bottom to clear sand from wrecks. Between them, I could just make out the name: *Reale*. Named after a Spanish coin and outfitted as she was, this was clearly more than a standard salvage vessel.

Standing on my board, I was eye level to the main deck and a quick glance revealed nothing. I called out and as I expected received no response. The smell of death hung over the boat and I hoped that between that and its being adrift I had just cause to board.

With my paddle in hand, I climbed over the gunwale and stood on deck. A set of dive gear lay off to one side with a collection bag, like the ones used to bag lobsters, next to it. Scattered pieces of black material were on the deck next to the bag. Carefully, I skirted the area and made my way to the cabin.

The smell almost drove me from the companionway. Using my sweaty shirt as a mask, I moved forward and stepped into the cabin. The shades were drawn over the small windows, making it hard to see, but something was down there and I knew what it was. Slowly, I stepped all the way inside and waited for my eyes to adjust. It didn't take long to make out the shape of a body on the V-berth. It lay face down on the bunk like it was asleep, but I guessed otherwise.

Reaching for the neck, I placed my hand by the carotid artery to check for a pulse. Cold dead skin greeted my touch and I pressed harder, hoping in vain that the man was alive. Finally, I pulled my hand away and stood back, leaning against the small sink on the other side of the cabin.

There was not a lot to think about at this point. I had been here before and knew what the protocol was. With my phone in Allie's care back on the beach, I went back up the steps to the cockpit and breathed in deeply before reaching for the microphone. Clicking the VHF on, I checked that it was on channel 16 and hailed the Coast Guard. They were the logical first responders and I had seen one of their vessels in the area working the race.

The dispatcher directed me to channel 19. I turned the dial and waited. A few seconds later her voice came through the speakers and asked what my emergency was. After giving her the details and our position from the GPS, I was advised to stand by.

If I'd had my phone, I would have called the medical examiner's office and started to document the site, but clad only in boardshorts and a Dri-Fit shirt, I had nothing to do but look around and wait. I moved to the transom, wanting to get as far upwind as possible from the smell. Sitting on the gunwale, I looked out to sea, wondering where the boat had come from. There were nothing but white-capped waves out there and I turned back to the bay to see where the boat was heading.

The water is all encompassing here, covering the spectrum of shades from a brilliant white to dark indigo and everything in between. If you know how to look, the variances tell a story. In this case they warned of shallow water and possibly a shoal ahead. The north wind was pushing us toward several patches of boat-killing brown water to the south of the channel. Moving forward, I stepped up on the top deck and made my way around the cabin to the bow. My plan was to set the anchor and secure the boat, but when I reached the windlass, I saw the white line already extended into the water. Leaning over, I pulled on it, not surprised when I met no resistance. About fifty feet of line lay on the deck when I reached the end.

The tendrils had unraveled, making it hard to see whether the line had snagged on something underwater or purposely been cut. I went with the latter explanation for now and set it aside for further examination. With no anchor to hold our position, I climbed back around to the helm and found the key still in the ignition. It was turned to off, indicating that the boat had been shut down manually.

The twin diesels started easily, belching a small black cloud from the exhaust. While they idled, I went to the stern and hauled my board onto the large back deck. Returning to the wheelhouse, I scanned the waters, set the throttle in reverse and backed the stern around, swinging the bow to open water. A boat was bearing down on my position, and I pushed the lever forward and steered in its direction. As the gap between us closed, I could see it was the Coast Guard vessel I had seen earlier.

Within minutes, our two boats were side by side.

"You say you have a dead body aboard?" the captain called from the helm.

"Yes, my name is Kurt Hunter, special agent with the National Parks Service."

He left the vessel in command of one of the crew and came to meet me across the gunwale. "I guess it's your report then. How can we assist?"

I explained about finding the boat adrift while I was racing, which explained my attire and lack of phone. "If I can borrow a phone, I'll call the medical examiner."

The captain handed me his phone. I wondered if I should check in with Martinez, my boss. His idea of the job description for special agent in charge was to observe through technology. In other words, he spied on his employees. Realizing that I had no phone and that I wasn't on the park service boat or truck gave me a strange sense of freedom from the three monitors that sat prominently on his desk. I decided I liked being invisible and would email him later rather than ruin his golf game.

I needed to start documenting things and glanced down at my watch that wasn't there. My report was going to be missing some key information, like what time I had found the body. The medical examiner was a no-brainer, though, and I dialed the number from memory, thinking while it rang that having the coroner's number in your head was not a good thing. Finally a man with a New Jersey accent answered.

"Sid, Kurt Hunter here."

"Greetings, special agent. Been fishing?"

I had found more than one body while fishing

the backwaters of the park. "No, out racing."

"And let me guess—"

"Yes, I found a body." I answered before he could complete his sentence.

"Of course you did. I wasn't expecting this was an invitation to go fishing."

The duo working the morgue were an odd pair, bonded by their interest in dead bodies and fishing. It worked for me as well, making it easy to connect with them. Though senior in both age and experience, Sid was the night and weekend guy. Vance, the hipster, was the head examiner. Both had hinted in their own way that they wanted or maybe expected me to take them fishing. I had taken Vance on a quick outing once and he had landed some fish, but also a duffle bag full of drugs.

My whole reason I had been assigned to Biscayne National Park was due to my passion for fishing. Previously stationed in the Plumas National Forest in Northern California, I had taken to explore the streams as I patrolled my area. Most of the action, at least during the warmer months, occurred around the water and I had carried a small collapsible fly rod with me, often stopping to cast to some of the trout in the streams. It was a great way to observe things and put my head in order.

There was something about the rhythm of the cast and retrieve that gave me a different perspective and I was able to see things I otherwise would have passed over. I had often found submerged dredges stashed underwater by illegal miners and in one case I had discovered a small eddy with a current running back toward a rock. Suspicious, I had removed the rock and discovered a pipe that had led me uphill to the largest pot grow ever found on public land. The cartel's response had been fast and hard, firebombing my house and breaking up my family. My posting here had been the park service's version of the witness protection program.

With my history of finding drugs and dead

bodies, I doubted a fishing expedition with the Miami-Dade medical examiners was a good idea. "Can you get out here?"

"Where is here?"

I gave him the coordinates. "Maybe I can bring the body to you." I didn't want to keep the Coasties around too long and with no anchor, it might be easier to run the boat into Miami. This would also leave the Miami-Dade police, who would have to transport Sid to the site with one of their boats, out of it—a worthy goal in any event.

We agreed on Dodge Island and I disconnected. "Okay if I call my daughter and I'll let you go?" I asked the captain.

He nodded. I looked down at the phone, trying to remember her number. I barely knew my own, but it came to me and I entered it into the dial pad hoping she would answer. The call went to voicemail and I left a brief message that I was okay and they should meet me at Dodge Island. A glance toward the finish line of the race showed the race was over except for a few stragglers. I knew Justine wasn't one of them and had probably finished. I left her a message as well, this one with a little more description.

After passing the phone back to the captain and explaining my intent, he ordered the crew to release the lines and I spun the wheel in the direction of the Miami Skyline, one of the two can't-miss navigational features of the park. With its low mangrove-lined shores the cluster of skyscrapers and to the south, the twin towers of the Turkey Point power plant were easy to spot. Once my course was set, I pushed the throttles. The heavy boat fought the engines and I finally gave up trying to get it to plane out. Backing off the power slightly, I plowed toward my destination.

The ride in gave me time to think. Sid would take the body, but after seeing the shredded anchor line, I needed a forensic opinion to rule out foul play.

That was where Justine came in. My new wife worked the swing shift as a tech for Miami-Dade. I hoped to get her to have a look without getting her in trouble.

The park service was notoriously slim on resources, which was one of the reasons Martinez and his budget-driven mentality flourished here. Without our own labs and techs we were reliant on the Florida Department of Law Enforcement and Miami-Dade for assistance. The FDLE's closest lab was in Tampa, too far for anything time-sensitive. That left Miami-Dade, and the Ivory Tower had set down the law: there would be no work for Kurt Hunter without a case number to charge it to.

I decided to take things one step at a time, safe in the knowledge that Martinez, unless he was listening to the VHF radio on the golf course, didn't know what had happened. I would get Justine's opinion and take it from there.

Because of the wind, once I crossed under the

Rickenbacker Causeway and entered the Intracoastal Waterway the boat traffic picked up. I wove my way through the afternoon cruisers until I saw the outline of two cruise ships that were moored at the port at Dodge Island. After finding an opening in the string of boats coming toward me, I cut through the traffic and headed to the small island.

Sid was ready and waiting on the dock. Because it had been built for commercial vessels it was always a challenge to dock my smaller center console here, but the larger boat, with its twin engines, was much easier to maneuver. With Sid's help, the boat was quickly tied off and secure.

"What'cha got down there? Smells like tuna," he called out over the engines.

I shut down the boat and looked up at him. Hunched over, the sun caught his bald spot and reflected back at me. He got down on one knee and then sat on the dock before swinging his legs over the side. I extended a hand to help, but he brushed it off and pushed himself down to the deck. With a questioning look he asked where the body was. I pointed to the cabin.

He stuck his head inside. "That's a big fish you got there, Hunter."

Chapter 3

Sid emerged from the wheelhouse. "There's no ID on the body."

I had chosen to wait in the fresh air on deck while he worked. I stopped short of commenting that I hadn't noticed any pockets in his wetsuit. "Are you ready to move the body?"

Like a windshield wiper in a downpour, he brushed the sweat from his brow onto the deck. "Okay, smart-ass. Maybe we'd better get some pictures and a time of death first—just in case." Beads of sweat had reappeared and his glasses slid down his nose as he gave me a look that meant I should be more respectful. "Care to join me?"

"I don't have my phone." I patted my boardshorts. He reached into his pocket, removed an oversized smartphone, and handed it to me. I pressed the *home* button and the screen lit up. "You really should have a password."

Again, his look answered me. "Just take the pictures."

I took several deep breaths and entered the wheelhouse. Moving from left to right, I started photographing the area where the body lay. Studying the scene through the phone's screen gave it a different perspective, allowing me to see things I had missed earlier. I carefully documented everything, noticing what looked like blood dripped on the floor. It was dry and looked old—probably fish blood—but I knew after being around Justine that any detail could be important. While I continued to document the site, Sid inserted the temperature probe into the man's liver.

"Okay?" I asked, handing Sid his phone as we exited the wheelhouse. "What'd you get for time of death?"

"Pretty fresh for one of your cases. I would

estimate between three and four hours. The heat in the cabin might skew things a little."

That put it between eight and nine this morning. While I had been getting ready for my race, he had died. "Ready to move him?"

"Me and you? That's a big boy in there." He grasped his lower back with one hand as he said it.

Sid had become a father figure and mentor to both Justine and me, and I never thought of him as old; more like a *Yoda* who defied age. From my inspection of the body, I estimated the man was over two hundred pounds—more than I could manage myself. We would need help and I looked around the docks. Because it was a Saturday, there was no one here; just the row after row of stacked cargo containers. There was probably someone across the island over by the cruise ships, but I wasn't sure I wanted a stranger involved. Sid gave me a questioning look, like I was holding him up from something important.

My choices seemed limited to calling Miami-Dade or waiting for Justine. Just as I was about to ask Sid to call for assistance, I heard the sound of a vehicle approaching and saw her car with the single board on top.

"What'cha got?" she called out of the open window.

My girl likes dead bodies. Not all that unusual for a forensics tech, but her fascination sometimes worries me. Allie leaned across her, anxious to see what was going on. That was going to be a problem. Her mom had been clear that I was to keep her away from my work.

I cocked my head at Justine. She understood and left the car. There was a smile on her face and a large medal on a white ribbon hanging around her neck. This was going to be a good day for her. Not only had she placed in her race, but now she had a dead body.

"Hey! Awesome job." I lifted the medal from

her chest, admiring it and wondering if I would ever get one of my own. "My race kind of got cut short. Got a body in the wheelhouse." I could tell from her smile that this was indeed turning out to be a banner day for her.

"Dad." Allie leaned across the driver's seat and called out the open window. "What's going on? Why didn't you finish?"

"Ran into a little problem."

"Is there a dead body on that boat?" she asked.

I had to figure out a way to deal with my teenager's morbid fascination. Lying was out of the question. She had been close to death before, when we'd been within a few hundred yards of the Highway 41 bridge collapse several months ago—but not this close.

"Yes. Why don't you wait there while Justine and I load it in the van?"

"I can help."

That wasn't going to happen. "We got it. Just

hang out there, okay." It was a statement, not a question.

Justine was already aboard, duplicating my efforts with her own phone. "You have a body bag?" I asked Sid. He came back with one and I brought it aboard. With Justine's help we bagged the body and carried it onto the deck. It was a bit of a struggle to move it up to the dock, but we did the best we could to preserve whatever dignity was left. A few minutes later the corpse was loaded into the medical examiner's van.

"See ya at the autopsy," Sid called out the window of the van. He assumed a hunched-over position, with his nose nearly touching the windshield, and accelerated. The wheels spun, kicking up the loose gravel in the lot, and he was gone.

I was glad Justine and Allie were here, if for no other reason than I didn't have to drive with him. Playing the Uber lottery was safer. With a squeal of tires, the van made a sharp turn and disappeared behind a stack of containers. The three of us stood there for a minute, staring at each other. "Can you have a look at something?" I asked Justine and motioned to the foredeck.

I followed as she hopped back down to the deck of the boat and we made our way around the wheelhouse to the bow. Allie was out of the car now, watching us. "Stay up there, okay. Don't want to contaminate the scene."

"Thanks, Dad," she snorted sarcastically and went back to the car.

I glanced back and saw her face buried in her phone. "Here." I reached down and grabbed the end of the anchor line.

Justine came toward me and pulled out her phone, taking a few pictures before she took the line from me. Slowly she turned it and brushed the frayed ends.

"Looks like you might have a crime scene," she said.

I couldn't tell if she was excited or upset that it had ruined our day. "What are you thinking?"

"It's cut for sure. It looks frayed because it unraveled in the water, but the ends are clean. If it had snagged on something they would be jagged. I'd say it was cut with a sharp knife."

I didn't know whether I was excited or upset. This was the first time we had all been together since our wedding. It had been a surprise and with Allie, Justine, and me floating behind the Interceptor after finishing a dive, Johnny Wells, my buddy from ICE had married us. The last few weeks before school started, and then Labor day, were busy weeks in the park, and Allie had asked for a few weekends to hang out with her friends. It had been hard to schedule time off together so we hadn't taken an official honeymoon. We had even talked about a family trip, but nothing had come together yet. A murder in the park would ruin what was left of what we'd expected to be a relaxing weekend.

I looked over at Allie and then Justine, trying to decide what to do. Generally I believe that momentum solves cases and I usually run full bore until they conclude. This tactic had gotten me in trouble with my family more than once, and I kept promising that I was going to put life before work. This appeared to be the perfect time to do that.

"It'll wait until Monday. I don't think anyone is going to mess with the boat here over the weekend and Sid has the body. Besides, we don't even know if a crime has been committed." I tried to justify my actions with the part of my brain that was ready to charge forward with an investigation.

That whole thought process was wasted when I saw the Miami-Dade Contender coming toward us with their light bar on. From a hundred yards out, I could see the man at the wheel and cringed. There was still enough time to get out of here before they arrived, but when I looked at Justine, she shook her head.

There was no love lost between the crew and me, and I remembered how they had leered at Justine. "If you want to disappear for a few, I'll handle these guys?"

I was both surprised and relieved when she agreed. Justine backs down to no one, sometimes to her detriment, but I got the feeling right now she was doing this for Allie and silently thanked her. A minute later her car pulled away and I turned back to the water.

The police boat approached the dock and slid in behind the converted sportfisher. I was a little envious of their approach until I remembered that they had a bow thruster, which made the maneuver easy. There was no point in being antagonistic right from the start so I walked over, ready to receive their lines.

Once the boat was secure, the captain disembarked with one of the crew—probably to reinforce his thug status.

"Well, look who it is, Ranger Rick," he said loud enough that the two other crew members still aboard could hear. "You ought to know better than to talk on the open airwaves."

There was no point in telling him that I'd had no choice. "What can I do for you?"

"Looks like you have a crime scene here. A little out of your jurisdiction, isn't it? And being that you're docked inside the city limits and all, that makes me curious."

"Found her adrift inside the park boundaries. Brought it over to make things easier on Sid." I regretted not hitting the *Man Overboard* button on the GPS to mark the location when I had come aboard.

"And where's Doey? Heard y'all got married."

I ignored the comment wondering if Justine was going to change her last name to mine to lose the nickname. Doeszinski could be a mouthful and the shortened versions were not flattering.

"Gotta follow procedures, Ranger boy. Should

have left her where you found the boat and called it in."

"The anchor line was cut. I'll call over and get it impounded if it makes you feel better."

"You know who this boat belongs to?"

There had been no ID on the man or time to find his identity. I had done a brief search for his phone and come up empty. Reluctantly I answered that I didn't. I did guess from the name *Reale* and the blowers hanging from the transom that it belonged to a salvor.

"That'd be Gill Gross."

He must have seen the blank look on my face.

"Treasure hunter. Been on TV and all for some of his finds."

And the answer to my question of why they were here was answered. I knew it was a work vessel from the boat's condition and from the way it was outfitted. By the way the two crewmen that had remained aboard the police vessel were eyeing the boat, I understood that there was more than a passing interest about Gross's demise and what might be aboard. Now that I knew who the dead man and owner were, the boat had to be protected, and I remembered the black chunks on the deck. I needed to get the crew out of here now.

I used the only card I had. "Grace Herrera has been notified and is on her way over."

"Could have said that up front." The captain backed away.

Grace was one of my only allies at Miami-Dade. We had worked together with some success on several other cases. She was level-headed, smart, and a knockout. She also had enough seniority to outrank this crew. The only problem with her was the friction between her and Justine that I couldn't figure out.

"If the she-monster is coming we better get on our way," he said loud enough that his crew heard.

The man standing behind him went for the lines and a minute later they were gone, idling away as if in defeat. The light bar remained off and their swagger seemed gone. Now I had to call Grace before my lie unraveled.

When Justine and Allie pulled up a minute later I retrieved my phone from my backpack. I heard the sounds of the approaching rotors of a helicopter and squinted into the sun. Even from this distance I could see the logo of one of the local networks on its sides. My call on the open airwaves of the VHF had been my only option at the time, and I realized that this case was not going to wait until Monday—it had just worked its way to the top of the priority ladder. Looking down at the screen, I found Grace Herrera's number and hit the phone icon.

Chapter 4

I wasn't sure if it was a good sign or not when the call went to voicemail. Grace was a talker, not a texter, so I left a vague message about what I had found and that the boat could potentially be a crime scene. After checking the water one more time to make sure Captain Ahab and his crew were gone I relaxed slightly, knowing that at least I had made an attempt to contact her.

The question now was what to do about the boat. Under normal circumstances there was little chance of anything happening to it at this location. I had left my park service boat here several times. But now I was concerned about the celebrity of its owner as well as his occupation.

"Thanks for handling Captain Nemo there," Justine said. For a few moments we both watched the helicopter hover overhead.

"Apparently this guy was a famous treasure hunter," I explained. "Nemo told me the boat's owner's a guy named Gill Gross. Ever hear of him?"

She shook her head. "What do you want to do about the boat, then? It probably needs to be processed quickly."

It was slightly comforting to know I wasn't the only one who had changed their priorities. And weather was always a consideration in South Florida. We were past the rainy season, but one stray squall would erase any evidence on the deck. "I was going to ask you. The last thing I want to do is work this weekend, but if this is really a crime scene we have to do something."

"I can help," Allie said.

Justine didn't object. I wasn't keen on making this a family operation, but with the two of them ganging up on me, I guessed that's what we were going to do.

My next decision was what to do with the boat. It clearly couldn't remain here. Miami-Dade had a boatyard they used for their own craft as well as impounded vessels, but I would lose access to it there. At least temporarily, I thought Adams Key might be the answer. The small island I lived on had two small park service houses; one was mine and Ray and his family occupied other. The long concrete dock, that also serviced the small day-use area, could easily handle our two boats plus Gross's. With a little luck, I could get it down there unobserved by both Miami-Dade and the media. Adams Key was fairly remote. The news helicopter was gone and I thought if I could get the boat out of here now, they would likely not find it. I also knew the workings of the local police department well enough to know that they wouldn't relent without a fight. If this were an unknown victim they would have no problem letting the case go, but this was going to be a media circus and whoever solved it would get the accolades.

Fortunately Martinez was a media hog as well—I knew he'd want this one for the park service. Removing the boat from their jurisdiction would work to that end as well.

"How about we run it down to Adams Key?" I explained my thinking.

"You two take her down. I'll run by the lab and get my kit. We can meet at the headquarters marina," Justine said.

"Really, Dad? That would be so cool." Allie tossed in her vote.

"Okay." I knew somehow that this was going to come back to haunt me, but if moving the boat to someplace less public held off the media for a few days it would be worth it. I hopped down on the deck, careful where I stepped, and went into the wheelhouse. Allie followed with a huge smile on her face, which quickly turned into a grimace when she smelt the lingering odor of the dead man from the cabin just forward of us.

I closed the hatch. "Once we're underway, it'll pass."

I started the engines and checked the gauges while Allie released the lines. There were two fuel tanks aboard and both appeared to be half full. I was sure the converted sportfisher had large tanks, but I didn't know their size and gas gauges on boats were notoriously inaccurate. Figuring it would be enough, I pressed down the throttles and steered the boat clear of the dock before turning to port. Once the bow was pointing toward the center span of the causeway, I took time to familiarize myself with the controls. Though only a dozen feet longer than my twenty-two foot center console, this boat was considerably wider and rode higher.

It was getting to be late in the afternoon now, and most boaters were heading back in from a day on the water. I asked Allie to keep out of sight when I saw several people raise their phones to take pictures of the unique looking vessel as we passed. I knew full well that once the death of Gross got out, these pictures would be all over the internet and I didn't want her to be in them.

Once past Cape Florida, the southern end of Key Biscayne, I decided to take the inside route. Even though the famed string of islands known as the Florida Keys officially began at Key Largo, the miles-long chain of barrier islands starting at Boca Chita Key were geologically the beginning of the ecosystem. The mangrove-covered islands and reefs that started in the park were indistinguishable from the Keys.

The ride became uncomfortable after passing Cape Florida. We were in unprotected water there and the boat was tossed around like a cork with the waves on our beam. Once we hit the shallows around Stiltsville the water flattened out, but the reprieve was short-lived and we hit another stretch of open water before gaining the lee of the barrier islands.

Once through the Featherbank Channel, I

turned toward the mainland and pointed the bow at the first marker leading to Bayfront Park. The large public boat park and our facilities, including the headquarters building, shared the same channel; after passing the ramp I cut the wheel to starboard and entered our small marina.

Johnny Wells's Interceptor was tied up in its usual place, as was the Florida Fish and Wildlife Commission's soft-sided boat used by Pete Robinson. Next were Susan McLeash's and my twin center consoles. Pulling up to the end of one of the finger piers we tied off the boat and sat back to wait for Justine.

Martinez's security cameras would surely have captured us by now and I tried to think of the best way to present this to him. I was big on asking for forgiveness instead of permission and thought sending him an after-the-fact, late Saturday email might accomplish that. I sat down with my phone, looking up every few seconds hoping to see Justine, and started pecking out a message. I kept the details vague and reread it several times as I knew he liked to parse words. It was as good as it was going to get and after a quick prayer that he wouldn't get it until Monday morning, I pressed *Send*.

Just as my phone chimed and the message went into the ether, Justine appeared by the back corner of the building. I stepped up to the dock to help her with the two large cases she had. From the determined look on her face I could tell she was taking this seriously. There would be no fun until she said so.

We loaded the equipment and pulled away from the dock. Catching the same looks from the incoming boaters as we had in Miami, I idled out of the channel. As soon as we passed the *Resume Normal Speed* placard, I pressed down lightly on the throttles. I didn't want to push the old boat too hard. I'd had trouble getting her up on plane earlier, so instead of forcing it we plowed toward Adams Key.

Any unfamiliar boat pulling up to the long concrete dock that serviced the small day-use area and the two houses on Adams Key was vetted by Zero. The pit bull mix that reminded me of Petey from the *Little Rascals* came bowling down the dock, barking as his toenails skidded on the concrete, stopping only a foot or so from my face. Aboard were his two favorite people. Cutting the ferocious dog act short, he plopped onto the dock and waited for the attention he knew was coming.

Allie was first off and she went directly to him. I watched as she squatted down next to him and started rubbing his ears. His tiny nub of a tail was working overtime as she spoke softly to him.

Ray must have seen the unfamiliar boat as well, and I watched as he came down the steps from his stilt house. He crossed the manicured lawn, one of the only leftovers from the notorious Cocolobo Club that had previously occupied our island. Opened in the thirties, the club had catered to four Presidents, the last being John F. Kennedy before shutting down in the sixties. Then hurricane Andrew's 140-mile-an-hour winds had erased whatever was left when the eye passed directly over the island in 1992. Now there were only our two park service-issue stilt houses and a couple of shade structures with grills in the day-use area.

"What'ch'all got going on there?" Ray asked.

"Kind of a long story, but I need to keep this here until Monday."

"Long story, huh," he said, stepping down to the deck of his boat. He opened the cooler in front of the console and returned with three beers. "Sorry, honey," he said to Allie. "Becky might have some Cokes up at the house."

"I'm fine, thanks. Dad's going to let me help process the boat."

That was more information than I wanted him to know.

"What y'all got going on, then?" He handed

beers to Justine and me.

I figured he'd find out soon enough and I knew I could trust him. Ray was the one guy on Martinez's payroll that had the leeway to do what he wanted, when he wanted to. Between the sun, heat, wind, and saltwater environment, Mother Nature did her best to reclaim the out islands. Ray knew how to tame her.

"Caught the boat drifting while we were racing. Dead guy aboard. Name's Gill Gross. Ever hear of him?"

"Treasure Hunter guy?" He looked at the boat differently now. "Shoot, he's all over the cable shows. Got any equipment aboard I can take a look at?" Ray asked, stepping closer to the boat.

If he was a barometer for how Gross's death was going to be received, I was in trouble. I didn't know if Gross had been a likable or charitable guy, but say the word *treasure* and it brings out something interesting in people—and it's often not good.

"Why don't you let Justine have at it first? When

she's done you can take a look."

He drained his beer and crushed the can. "Got out and snagged some snapper today if you want to barbecue later."

In all the excitement I hadn't thought about food. Since we had been married, Justine and I spent almost every night together, but we were forced by logistics to keep two residences. The house here was definitely better provisioned than when I'd lived alone, but we had planned on eating out to celebrate the race tonight.

"Lemme check with the boss," I said, tilting my head toward Justine.

"See you're learning." He laughed. "All right then, let me know."

Zero and I watched him walk upstairs. I looked down at Allie and the dog and I smiled, watching them playing together.

"Get some help?" Justine called out, breaking the spell.

Zero followed as we both went over to the edge of the dock. Justine held a black object about half the size of a bowling ball in her hand.

"I think he found something."

"Cannonball?" Allie asked.

"I don't know. It's pretty irregular."

I hopped down to the deck and, avoiding the two cases' worth of gear scattered across the stained surface, moved to where Justine was standing. She handed me the object. My first impression was how light it was. The second, when I spun it in my hands, was how much the material looked like what I had seen scattered on the deck.

"You see this stuff here?" I asked, walking toward the stern.

"Freeze. I haven't gotten there yet. I'm still in the cabin."

I had already crossed this section of deck earlier, but I was not going to disobey. "Look at this stuff." I pointed this time. "The outer covering looks like that stuff. I think he found more than cannonballs."

"Can we open it up?" Allie asked.

I wasn't sure what the answer to that was and looked at Justine for help. In my view it was worthless as evidence until we found out what was inside.

"We're going to need to get the state involved. If there is something valuable with historic significance, they're going to want to know."

That was my worst-case scenario. As an employee of the federal government, I knew exactly how bureaucrats could muck things up and stall an investigation.

Chapter 5

The mood was restrained as we sat around Ray's customized park service grill that evening. A hundred feet away, the *Reale* seemed to have cast a strange spell over the island. The scene of a man's death also held the potential for riches; it was both morbid and exciting at the same time.

The charcoal and wood mixture that Ray preferred crackled beneath the stainless steel grate he had fabricated for the standard fire ring common to most national parks. Two rods welded to the base on either side made the detachable grill easier to handle than the original cast-iron piece. Becky turned the corn, still in its husk, that sat next to the snapper Ray had caught earlier.

The object that was sitting on the counter in my

kitchen had affected us all. As much as I tried to rise above it, I was still under the spell of the potential treasure.

"When can we look at it?" Becky finally asked.

"Y'all know it ain't nothing 'til we see what it is," Ray added.

"Yeah, Dad," Allie called over from where she was playing with their three-year-old son Jamie.

I looked at Justine, who seemed to be deep in thought. She looked tired, but that was probably the result of the race earlier. Working the swing shift for the forensics lab, she was used to a late morning nap after training. That schedule had been interrupted today.

She shrugged, leaving it up to me. I wanted to know what was inside the sphere as well, and the thought of having it disappear into some state inspector's grasp bothered me. For as long as man had been going to sea, ships had been lost and attempts had been made to salvage them. I understood the need to protect our history, but the sea was a cruel caretaker and not a museum.

"Can we see what is inside without damaging it?" Three sets of eyes focused on her.

"I've seen them do it on TV. It's not rocket science, but you have to be patient."

Allie handed her phone to me and I felt like I had fallen into a trap. Playing on the screen was a YouTube video of someone with a similar object, about to break it open. "Whatever is inside, we can't keep it." I wanted to establish some ground rules first.

"No problem. Just curious is all," Ray said.

I could see something else in his eyes. It wasn't greed; more like a calculated look. Although we had it pretty good, living out here rent-free in our park service homes, he was younger than I was and I suspected Becky might be pregnant again. If not, I knew they were at least planning on more children. Once Jamie reached school age, this would probably mean relocating to the mainland so he could attend school. Living out here meant anywhere from a twenty to a forty-five-minute boat ride into headquarters and then whatever commute from there. Some days the weather didn't permit our small bay boats to get out at all. Moving would mean he would have to pay rent, and knowing Martinez, there would be no salary increase to compensate. I knew Ray profited from a string of lobster and stone crab traps that he strategically located just outside of the park boundary in areas he knew to be in the migratory path of the crustaceans. That and his fishing supplemented his income, but I wondered if it was enough.

The video finished and I handed the phone to Justine.

Justine looked up when it was over. "I don't have the stuff to do that here. It needs to soak in muriatic acid and then sit in an electrolysis tank. That takes time."

I could see the downcast looks. We were all curious. "From the pieces on the deck, it looks like someone took a hammer and chisel to something similar."

"I suppose that could remove the outer covering, but I don't want to touch whatever is inside. That should be done by a pro."

None of us had any idea how to proceed, but finally our curiosity won and we negotiated a strategy. Each of us had our own reasons for wanting to see what was inside: Allie was curious, Justine was fascinated by the archeological and scientific implications of the find, and—hoping it wasn't greed—I was still trying to figure out Ray's motivation. I, of course, was only looking for clues, or at least that was my story.

Once we agreed on how to proceed, we ate quickly and gathered around the bar in my kitchen, staring at the object that lay on a baking sheet by the sink. Justine put on gloves, picked it up, and held it to the light to see if there were any points of weakness. Allie picked up my phone and started to video the procedure. I reached over and grabbed it from her. Filming this would be bad for everyone and using my phone would be worse; the Cloud would place the video on Martinez's desktop.

"Let's keep this between ourselves," I said.

Justine set the object on the tray again and with a small pick that looked like it had come from a dentist's office started removing tiny fragments. As she found weaknesses in the coating of silt and marine growth that had hardened into a concrete-like shell, bigger chunks slowly started to come off. After several passes, the chunks on the tray started to resemble what lay on the deck of the boat and we all gathered closer.

One by one pieces fell from the object. Suddenly she stopped and put it down on the tray. Removing a magnifying glass from her case, she picked up a piece and held it to the light. From where we sat we couldn't see what she was looking at, and collectively we held our breath.

"I think there's silver or something," she said. She showed each of us, one at a time, what she had found. A small glint of metal had appeared inside the dark crusty casing. "That's it for me. This is going to a pro."

I guessed that everyone else was feeling the same mix of excitement and disappointment as I was.

"That was the deal," I said, restating what we had all agreed on.

While Justine placed the find in an evidence bag, Ray and family said their good-byes. As they left I tried to make eye contact with him, but each time I did his gaze shifted away.

An hour later, I stared at the ceiling in my bedroom. Justine was snoring softly, sound asleep beside me.

I had discovered a strange phenomenon during my time here: though I hadn't confirmed it, I suspected that all boat owners had some kind of built-in radar about their vessels. While boats and cars both got you from one place to another, they were totally different animals. Once you parked and locked a car, it would take an experienced thief to break in or steal it. But with a boat, there were tides, currents, storms, lines, and a myriad of other factors that affected it at dock. Over the last year, something in my subconscious had woken me several times in the middle of the night, alerting me to check the boat. Each time there had been an adjustment needed or a problem to be addressed.

I had the same feeling now. Knowing sleep was not coming, I slid from the bed, careful not to wake Justine. Out on the porch, which overlooked the dock, I could see a dim light coming from the wheelhouse of the *Reale*. My first thought was that there was a good chance when I'd been trying to familiarize myself with the controls of the boat, I had inadvertently flipped a switch. The daylight would have prevented me from seeing the light was on. That theory went out the window when I saw a shape pass in front of it.

After retrieving my mag light and weapon from inside, I slipped into my flip-flops and eased open the screen door. It gave its usual squeak as it closed and I froze in place until I was sure it hadn't been noticed. One at a time, I took the stairs down to the walk, careful to put my weight on the outside of the treads where they were less likely to make noise. On reaching the concrete walkway, I paused again. There was still no indication that I had been spotted and I scanned the dock to see if there were any strange boats nearby. Unless they had tied off to the outside of the treasure boat, I couldn't see an intruder, and when the shape moved again I saw the profile. I had no doubt it was Ray.

I didn't want a confrontation with my only neighbor, but I had to see what he was doing. If we were going to have a face-to-face, I might as well let him know I was here. I knew he had at least a rifle and sneaking up on him might prove fatal.

"Hey," I called out softly as I approached the dock. I saw a shadow cross the light again and a second later Ray appeared on the deck.

"Just making sure she was secure," he said.

Standing with his hands on his hips, his body language told me otherwise. "I had the same feeling. Did you check the lines?"

"All good." He went back into the wheelhouse and shut off the light, then reappeared on deck. "Think I'll head back up to bed."

We exchanged wary glances as he passed me on the walkway. "Think I'll have a look as well."

There was no point in waiting for him to disappear into his house; I suspected he would be watching me. As badly as I wanted to go into the wheelhouse and see if there was any evidence of what he had been doing, I casually checked the cleats to make sure the lines were secure, then after adjusting the spring line—though it didn't need it—I hopped down to the deck. I glanced back at Ray's house and noticed that most of the boat would be obstructed from his view. He would see a light, but as long as it stayed dark, he couldn't see what I was up to.

It was a dark night with only a crescent moon above. A security light on the dock cast a shadow but did little to illuminate the deck. I wondered if the surveillance camera Martinez had mounted above the pole had night vision. Viewing the video to see what Ray had been doing would require either a stealth operation to get into his office or having to ask him outright. Neither option appealed to me.

Staying in the shadows, I moved toward the wheelhouse and entered the dark space. Looking around at the instruments, I tried to figure out what Ray had been doing. It didn't take long when I saw the GPS unit mounted above the dashboard. In the treasure hunting and salvage world, those numbers were invaluable. Tomorrow, before we did anything else, I would check the unit.

Ray was someone I knew and trusted, but seeing how his behavior had changed when the word *treasure* was used and when he had seen the glint of silver put me on high alert. He wouldn't be the only one, either. Once the media ran the story and found out where the boat was docked, I expected visitors.

I left the boat and walked back to the house. It was quiet when I entered, but I knew sleep was not coming quickly. Unplugging my laptop from the charger, I sat on the couch and started Googling anything that might help me understand what Gross would have been after.

An hour later, my eyes were starting to close. As can be the case with the internet, there was too much information: forums, articles, and books flooded my search results. After looking, bleary-eyed, at my pages of random notes, I hoped that the GPS would tell me more in the morning and went back to bed.

Chapter 6

I woke Sunday morning to the smell of pancakes. The sound of Justine and Allie talking in the kitchen bled through the walls, above the background noise of what I guessed was the TV. Sunlight streamed in through the edges of the blackout shades I had recently installed at Justine's request. We were still adjusting to our two-home lifestyle and I wanted to do anything that would make her more comfortable here. I had to admit planning our new life had been fun, and as I listened to the hum of conversation, I lay there happy. Then, groggy from lack of sleep, I slowly climbed out of bed and dressed in cargo shorts and a t-shirt. My standard Sunday wear was not that much different from my day-to-day uniform of khaki shorts and a park service polo. After throwing some water on my face, I brushed my teeth and headed out for some food and coffee.

The girls had breakfast ready and I eagerly dug in. Allie wanted to know what we had planned and I searched my brain for a half-day activity that would end by three, when we would need to leave to get her home on time.

I had quickly learned that one of the keys to a stable relationship with my ex was to be timely for exchanges. Monday through Friday Allie lived with her mom, an arrangement I had agreed to for my daughter's benefit. Stability was important, especially for a teenager, and though I missed some milestones of her growing up, it was the best thing for her.

"What do you guys want to do?"

"Justine said I could help her process the rest of the boat," Allie said.

I looked over at Justine, who nodded and then glanced out the window. You didn't need a degree in meteorology to forecast the weather here. Described as seven months of summer and five months of hell, what we were currently in might be considered purgatory. October had as equal a chance of tropical weather as cold fronts, but as the year faded into November, the tropics cooled down and the cold fronts became stronger. It was rare for one to reach this far south and even when it did, it was generally mild. December and January brought those dreaded fifty-degree days when the down coats, hats, and gloves came out.

A light breeze rustled the palm trees. From their movement I gauged the wind at five to ten miles per hour from the southeast—a typical early fall day. "It looks pretty good out there. You sure you don't want to go fish or something?" I was making every effort not to sabotage what was turning out to be the best time in my life by letting work interfere.

"I really want to help," Allie said, making things easier.

"If you're sure. Maybe if you guys finish we can

try and find that school of juvenile tarpon that's been hanging around." Chico, one of the local guides I had befriended, had turned me on to the spot across Caesar Creek, where the school hung out on the falling tide. My experience out west had been fly-fishing the streams, but lately I had been converted to spinning gear, mostly for the ease and ability to fish deep enough for the snapper and grouper that were plentiful here if you knew where to look. Tarpon was a catch-and-release fish, and I had been teaching Allie and Justine how to fly-fish for them. Even though you couldn't eat them, the blazing runs and jumps of the ten to fifteen-pound fish made them fun to catch.

I'd made my offer, and if CSI was what they wanted to do I was all for it. I was also getting anxious about who else might be looking for the *Reale*. My fears turned the corner to reality when I saw a picture of the same boat we had docked outside on the TV screen.

"Hold on," I said, going for the remote. The three of us stared at the screen.

"Treasure hunter Gill Gross was found dead aboard his boat the *Reale* yesterday," the on-screen reporter said. The screen changed to show a group of people around another boat with a mailbox attached to its stern. The similarities ended there. This one was at least twice the size of Gross's boat and looked much newer. "We're here with several of Gross's friends. Let's get their reaction." The reporter approached a man. From a glimpse of his body language, I could tell he held himself in high regard. He puffed out his chest and I thought he might have done a tippy-toe rise to appear larger. "With me is one of Gross's contemporaries, Vince Bugarra."

It was clear after listening to the interviews that the media didn't have much information. But that was likely to change. I could only hope that Martinez had an early tee time and hadn't seen the news.

"This might be our last shot at that boat without

having the media and who knows who else looking over our shoulders," Justine said.

"Okay." I wanted to have a look at the electronics anyway. "While you guys do your thing, I think I'll try and download the GPS data and see if we can figure out where he was."

"Really," Justine said in surprise. "Thought that up all by yourself? I must be rubbing off on you." She reached over and punched my arm.

I hadn't told her about Ray's visit to the boat last night and didn't plan on it, at least while Allie was around. It was Ray's interest that had given me the idea. Moving to the junk drawer by the refrigerator I pulled a bundle of tangled cables out and set them on the counter, then with my laptop in hand, I grabbed the pile and headed out the door.

I had decided not to confront Ray about his clandestine visit before at least looking at the data. When I saw that his boat was gone, the point appeared to be moot. I could only hope he wasn't heading for trouble. Then again, knowing Ray, he could just as easily be out fishing, checking his lobster traps, or setting his stone crab traps. Looking at my watch, I saw it was the fifteenth, stone crab opening day. Storms had turned last year's season into a disaster, but I had been around the water long enough to know that conditions could change on a dime. There had been a lot of talk amongst the commercial guys about scaling back their operations or not setting traps at all this year, but I knew they would. You weren't going to win if you didn't enter.

It was actually a relief that he was gone and I dropped down to the deck of the boat and brought my laptop and the bundle of cables into the wheelhouse. I wasn't the park IT guy, but I knew my way around computers and electronics, so hooking up the computer to the GPS was well within my skill set. After studying the unit, I saw I was halfway there without even plugging in and reached to open a small cover where a micro SD card could be inserted. It was empty. My thoughts turned to Ray and I wondered if he had taken it. The benefit of the doubt I'd been giving him would be revoked if he had.

The GPS on the park service boats was simpler than the unit aboard the *Reale*, but the concept was the same. Pressing the power button, I waited for the unit to acquire the satellite signals and started scrolling through the screens. Allie and Justine had come on board now, but I ignored them as I familiarized myself with the unit.

I already knew that the SD card was not the entire memory, just a supplement. After finding the waypoints page, I scrolled through the screen, finding over a hundred points. To export them to my computer I would need to connect to the unit, so I searched through the cables to find one that would fit. Several times I was frustrated, but I finally found it. Now I had to export the data.

Scrolling to the data screen, I found the export to KML option and touched the screen to select it.

Touchscreens were fairly new on marine GPSs and I got a little equipment envy when I saw how much faster they worked than the one aboard my center console. The computers acknowledged each other and the data was soon confirmed on my laptop.

The numbers on the unit were a shot in the dark. Fishermen were notorious for guarding their hard-earned numbers; with what was at stake, I had to assume treasure hunters were even more hardcore. I expected that the numbers stored on the machine were mostly public marinas and reefs; all available on the internet.

Before long I had everything I could get from the GPS and decided that the temptation was too great to leave the unit aboard. After unscrewing it from the base, I removed the wires in the back and set it with the laptop. Justine and Allie were still working on the deck and I noticed the dive gear still where I had found it yesterday.

"Can we look at the gear?" I asked.

"I'd like to have a quick look, but if it was used yesterday, the saltwater probably erased any evidence," Justine said.

This brought my thinking back to the cause of death. Sid worked weekends and I pulled out my phone and texted him. Hopefully he would postpone the autopsy until we had dropped off Allie. I would have rather sat on the couch and watched football, but with the publicity this case was already garnering I wanted to make sure I was there.

He answered that he would wait and start at four. I replied that we would be there. There was no need to ask Justine. My new wife had a preference for the dead over the living. I looked back toward them; they were working the area where the concretions were. I watched Allie squat and use a pair of tweezers to place the small chips in an evidence bag.

Justine rose and walked toward the gear. I allowed her space, knowing she hated to have anyone looking over her shoulder. She was an experienced diver and knew her way around the equipment better than I did, so I stood back and watched.

After taking a slew of pictures and making a thorough visual inspection, she checked her gloves and reached for the regulator. Pressing the purge button did nothing. Next she checked the air gauge and the tank valve.

"Empty."

"We've been there; that's not that unusual." I was an air hog, especially compared to Justine. We all knew it was bad practice, but on several shallow water dives where the boat had been visible and directly above us, I had pushed the envelope and run out of air trying to extend the bottom time.

"There's no indication that anyone was with him." She looked at the empty tank racks.

I looked at the yellow and green band around the tank that labeled it as suitable for NITROX. The oxygen-rich mix helped extend bottom time. There was always the chance he had gotten a bad mix, but with an empty tank there was no way to prove it. The cause of death would have to wait for Sid's determination.

"You guys about done?" I asked, looking at my watch. Commuting from an island involved more than traffic. With the weather holding and the seas down, I expected the run to headquarters would take about twenty minutes. Then Miami traffic would come into play. We needed to leave in about a half hour to allow enough of a cushion to meet Allie's mom on time. I went back to the wheelhouse and grabbed my computer and the GPS unit.

"Where you going with that?" Justine asked.

"Just removing temptation. I'll give it to the next of kin."

"It should be dusted for prints."

Pretending to fumble with the unit, I rubbed the screen against my shirt. As a federal employee, Ray would have his prints on file. As the last person besides me to touch the unit, his name would turn up if she ran them. Still not sure what to do with him, as his neighbor and friend I decided to protect him. I shrugged, promising myself to tell her later about his late-night visit.

Chapter 7

Though it's not listed on *Yelp*, if you want a surefire remedy for the South Florida heat and humidity, I can recommend the coldest place in town. Because of the high water table and storm surges most buildings here are built on fill, but the Miami-Dade Medical Examiner's office is located in one of the only basements in Dade County. Looking down at the body, I shivered from the cool air blowing on the back of my neck from the oversized ventilation system. The sterile room, with tiled walls and floor and stainless steel everything else, did little to provide any warmth. I felt goose bumps on my arms as I stood on the far side of the table watching Sid and Justine examine the body.

I'd been lucky so far with the few autopsies I had attended. My first cases had involved bodies that had been in the water. The longer the saltwater and sea life had to attack the body, the more clinical it appeared on the table. In comparison, Gill Gross looked fresh, although there were some signs of his death. His skin, which I remembered as having the deep tan of someone who spent his life outdoors, had turned a pallid grey overnight. Now, more than twenty-four hours after his death his muscles had slackened to the point that he looked like a rag doll. In layman terms he was no longer a stiff.

Sid was just about done with the anterior inspection.

"Think you can help us roll him?" he called across to me.

In many police departments investigators are required to attend the autopsy. In my three-person office there was no such rule and no chance Martinez or Susan McLeash would ever cross the threshold of the sterile room. As much as I didn't care to be here either, I had learned the value of observation. The medical examiner's priorities were to identify the deceased and find the cause of death. They often overlooked things that could lead to the killer. There were of course detailed reports, but reading through the mundane verbiage it was easy to miss details.

Unlike many investigators, who never looked forward to being present at an autopsy, Justine could do this every day. She eagerly assisted Sid whenever she could. The old Jersey transplant had been doing this since Justine and I had been in diapers, and though forensics had changed drastically over those years, a dead body was still a dead body, and Sid knew his way around one.

I moved to the other side of the table and helped them roll Gross's body. Sid started his observations at the top of the scalp and moved down through the body, noting every detail as he went. I soon tired of the monotone dictation and started looking ahead. Unfortunately, I saw nothing that was going to get me out of the internal portion of the procedure that was soon to follow.

I had assumed correctly and we took a short break before he made the Y-shaped incision that would allow him access to the internal organs.

"You don't have to sit through this," Justine said. "I'll give you a full update."

"I better stay," I said, thinking about the football game that was coming on any time now that I would rather be watching.

"Okay. We can watch the game later. I taped it."

I leaned in and kissed her.

"When you two lovebirds are done, I'd like to get back to it."

We walked back into the cold room and waited while he opened up the body. My gag reflex was primed and ready to go, but not needed. Whether the body had been transferred to one of the refrigerated cases lining the walls fast enough to arrest its bloating, or I had become hardened to the smells of death, there was little putrid gas coming from the body and I relaxed.

Without having to worry about losing my lunch, I watched as Sid removed the man's organs, commented, weighed, and placed them in jars. I heard something that caught my attention when he removed the lungs and heart. Between the Latin and scientific terms I caught some English that I understood. The words *embolism and heart failure* stood out.

"We found the tank empty. Could he have shot to the surface and died?"

"It seems likely. I'll order a CT scan of his brain, but I would rule the cause of death as a diving accident if I was asked right now."

"What if you weren't asked right now? The anchor line looked like it had been cut with a knife and there was evidence that something is missing."

"And you want me to delay my findings?"

"Just until you get the test results back."

"I can do that, but Vance will be in tomorrow

morning and see the reports. I'm off Monday and Tuesday so he'll be releasing the cause of death."

"Appreciate it." I made a mental note to swing by in the morning and promise Vance a fishing trip.

Occam's Razor states that the simplest answer is usually the correct one. This may work with live people, but from my experience it rarely worked with a homicide. I started to organize the case in my head as I watched Sid and Justine methodically complete the interior section of the autopsy and move to the head.

To me, cases are like jigsaw puzzles. You have to start with the corners—which I label motive, opportunity, means, and a trigger incident that allows everything to happen—and then work on the border. It all seemed too easy. Killing a treasure hunter for what he had found, or more likely where he had found it, was a slam-dunk for a motive. Gross being underwater when he heard the sound of a boat above could have forced him to rush to the surface, where he died of an embolism.

Motive, means, and opportunity all wrapped up in a neat bundle—too neat, and too easy, but enough to start an investigation. Now all I had to do was convince Martinez this was worth pursuing.

An hour later, sitting on the couch watching the game with Justine, my mind kept spinning with the loose ends I couldn't place. Why was the tank empty? Where was the SD card and why had Gross been diving alone in rough weather? The only thing I could guess with any probability of being correct was that the anchor line had been cut to hide the position of whatever Gross had been diving on.

I was distracted throughout most of the football game. California had its problems, but Pacific time was a blessing for sports fans. Games that started at eight on the east coast aired at five on the west, making for a much better sleep schedule. Just after eleven, a time I would normally be asleep but instead was still up and cursing east coast sports, my phone rang.

My Monday morning wakeup call had been accelerated—Martinez's name flashed across the display. There was no point in antagonizing him and I took the call, thinking he intended to leave a voice message. The disruption worked, but didn't throw him off his game for long.

"What the hell, Hunter?"

Apparently, his usual good morning salutation also meant good night.

"Have you seen the news?" he asked.

I paused the recorded game and flipped through the channels, finding nothing. He must have seen earlier reports.

"Are you there?" Martinez said loudly enough that Justine could hear.

"I sent you an email with all the details as of last night."

"I haven't seen it."

I had been right in assuming that he didn't

forward his work emails to his phone. When Martinez was off the clock he was off. That gave me a slight advantage. "I found a boat adrift in the park yesterday. The treasure hunter, Gill Gross, was aboard and dead."

"And the location of the boat?"

"I brought it out to Adams Key. With all the publicity that this is going to get, I didn't want it in Miami."

"And yet you're in Miami."

He knew my location from the tracker on my phone. That fact was one of the larger holes in my plan. "Ray is keeping an eye on it and we just finished the autopsy a few hours ago."

"Cause of death?"

"Looks to be an embolism from surfacing too quickly. My theory is that he had been underwater when someone came by his boat and cut the anchor."

"That's not a murder, Hunter. And if you don't have definitive proof that the anchor was cut there is no foul play here. Once again you've crossed the line."

I thought he had crossed a line as well, calling this late on a Sunday night. "I am available tomorrow morning if you'd like to meet." I set it out like bait, hoping for a response.

"Evaluations are due soon, Hunter. I'd watch yourself."

Like that was going to faze me. "Right. See you at eight." I disconnected before he could answer. Eight was at least a half hour earlier than he typically got to work. Hopefully that would play to my advantage. He'd be mad for sure, but I didn't care about that. I wanted him unprepared.

The game was over with ten minutes left on the clock, and rather than succumb to more of the announcer's trite comments I grabbed Justine off the couch and took her to bed.

Chapter 8

My phone rang and I reached over to grab it. My first mistake of the day was answering without looking at the caller ID.

"We're wanted on the news," Martinez said.

I struggled to open my eyes and when I did saw it was still dark out. Justine rolled away from me and covered her head. Most days she would be out training, but she had graciously given us a week off following the race. Whether she was able to keep that promise was yet to be seen.

The call from Martinez had me wide awake and I listened as he gave me the address of the TV station.

"This is big, Hunter. Don't let me down."

Before I headed to the shower I found a clean

uniform. Taking it with me into the bathroom, I started the shower and hung it on a hook, hoping the steam would take some of the wrinkles out. Martinez had sounded even more excited than usual. He lived for the cameras, but I had never been asked to appear with him. I knew the network and guessed this wasn't your standard press conference—this was an interview on the biggest morning show in South Florida.

Apparently news of the treasure hunter's death had spread quickly, making Martinez happy and me anxious. I had only appeared before news cameras once before, out in California. The exposure from that interview had put me front and center, in the cartel's sites, finally resulting in the firebombing of our house and the subsequent custody hearing that took Allie away from me for over a year.

I kissed Justine on the head as I left the bedroom and debated whether to tell her where I was off to. Putting my anxiety aside, I told her to watch channel four at eight o'clock.

She popped her head out of the covers. "What the hell?"

Martinez's morning greeting sounded strange coming from her. "Martinez called and said to be there. They want to interview me."

"Awesome. I'll set up the DVR. You should let Allie know."

I kissed her again and left thinking about Allie, deciding it was better to show the interview to her later, when I was sure there would be no fallout from it. There was also the issue of Jane seeing it, and that might not be good for what I hoped would stay a relatively peaceful custody agreement. I still had two years to survive until Allie was eighteen and could make her own decisions.

Leaving Justine's place, I headed downstairs to the truck, got in, and entered the address Martinez had given me into my phone's map app. The phone seemed to know where I was going and displayed a picture of the network's building. I hit *GO* and left the parking lot. With increasing anxiety, I followed the directions through the quiet streets to the station.

There was no sign of Martinez when I arrived, giving me a few minutes to decide how to play this. Publicity was not my thing; it was his. That was possibly the only attribute that made our relationship tenable at all. I decided to wait for him and let him take the lead, both because I didn't want to deal with the network producers alone and because doing so might pay dividends down the road.

While I waited, I took out my pad and started making some notes. I had found the body, and now with the network coverage there would be little doubt that it was my case. That made me responsible for officially notifying the next of kin. They most likely already knew, but murders, if this was one, were usually committed by someone the victim had known. That put his family on top of the suspect list.

My list would grow. Justine had found his cell

phone aboard, which was now bagged and tagged with the rest of the evidence she had collected yesterday. I hoped the messages and call log it contained would help me establish a timeline for the last hours of his life. Then there was the GPS information stored on the phone, and I made a note to contact the cell provider to get the locations of Saturday's calls and messages. Unlike the park and the Keys, where you had to travel five miles to the reef before finding deep water, South Florida's topography was different and dropped off quickly from shore. A hundred feet of water lay less than a mile offshore, in easy cell range. But I wasn't getting my hopes up. Based upon Saturday morning's wind direction and current Gross had likely been more to the southeast, where there was little cell service, and that was if his phone was on at all.

The GPS information from his unit was less promising, but still needed a better look. That was something that I was familiar enough with to work on my own. I didn't think it would reveal his honey hole, but there might be something there.

There was still no sign of Martinez when I put aside the list and picked up my phone. Googling Gill Gross, I scanned through the results, trying to gauge the shit show that was bound to follow the interview. The first two pages of results were reports of his death. Finally I started to see results about his life.

Leaning back in the seat, I watched a video of an interview he had done about six months ago. I wasn't sure what I'd expected, but despite his weather-worn look, he appeared optimistic. Video showed what looked like some large urns, still intact, then the camera continued along the wreck, showing a cannon and some ballast. It looked like stock footage and there was no mention of the wreck's origin or history, only a plea for funding.

Just as the video ended, Martinez pulled up next to me. I got out of my truck and met him on the sidewalk. After a quick appraisal of my uniform he nodded and I followed him inside. We gave our names to the receptionist and were introduced to a bubbly intern who led us back into the guts of the station. I tried to remember the turns we made in case I needed a quick escape, but by the time she left us alone in a dressing room, I had to admit I was lost.

"Just follow my lead," Martinez said, checking his face for blemishes in a magnified makeup mirror. Finding something he didn't like, he reached for some kind of powder and touched up the spot.

"I did a little research. Gross was a big deal. Looks like he might have fallen on hard times, though. There's a lot out there about him needing funding." I thought I ought to give him a heads up before we were confronted on camera. He thanked me for the briefing and I saw in his eyes that this might be an opportunity for the park, but I knew it was more about his personal advancement. I saw it as a minefield.

He continued with the appraisal of his face in

the mirror until someone knocked on the door and then entered. The woman looked familiar and by her makeup and dress, my finely honed investigative skills told me she was the talent.

"I'm Haley Brenton," she said proudly.

I'd never heard of her, but Martinez jumped up and shook her hand.

A man, clearly her handler from his disheveled appearance, stood behind her with a clipboard. Introductions were made and another woman entered and directed me to the chair next to Martinez. I squirmed as she fussed with my hair and applied powder to my face. Martinez seemed happy with the attention; where I was a victim of her ministrations, he was directing her.

They told us we had about twenty minutes and left the room. I felt foolish with the bib around my neck and pulled it off. Martinez continued to examine his face. Finally satisfied, he turned to me.

"We need to be very careful here, Hunter. Is

there really a crime?"

The question surprised me. He typically resisted every case I put in front of him. "Forensics is pretty conclusive the anchor line was cut. The autopsy showed the cause of death as a heart attack that was likely caused by an embolism. That's the grey area. His tank was empty, but that is far from conclusive."

"Best stick to the facts and leave your theories out of it for now."

The *for now* was promising. "What do you want to do about his boat?" I asked.

"Until it's a problem, let's bring it to headquarters. There are a few empty slips there and I have surveillance in place."

I tried not to laugh, but his paranoid measures might pay off now. I didn't really want the boat at Adams Key, but there was little to stop anyone from boarding it at the marina. The park headquarters did have a few gates that could block the roads, but there was nothing to stop a boat. At least his cameras would tell us who had been there.

"Let's announce that there was no evidence on the boat," he decided.

"I removed the GPS; putting that out there might mitigate any problems."

"Good idea," he said.

There was another knock on the door and someone called out a five-minute warning. I knew this truce with Martinez was too good to last so I decided to firm up my position.

"I'm going to need to bring in some resources to help with some of the technical aspects. A diving and salvage specialist could really help."

"Experts are expensive."

At least he still had an eye on his budget.

"I have a few guys that I could bring in on the side. I doubt they'll testify in court, though," I told him. My first case here had led me to the Keys, where I'd met TJ, his wife Alicia, and Mac Travis. Between TJ's diving prowess and Travis's salvage experience, I thought they could help, but there was no way either would testify if something developed that ended up in court. Travis was a recluse and TJ's dive business was a cover for his and Alicia's work as contractors for the CIA.

He nodded, giving me his unspoken blessing that I knew could be revoked at any time. "Keep it off the books."

Another knock on the door interrupted our conversation. This time it opened and we were led down a hallway into a brightly lit set. We were instructed to sit in two chairs set before a low table with empty coffee cups on top of it. Martinez, of course, took the one closest to the host's seat. We sat waiting while adjustments to the microphones and cameras were made. It had been only a few minutes and I was already starting to sweat under the hot lights when the woman came in and sat next to Martinez.

"Ready in five," a voice that was lost in the

bright lights called out.

He counted down to one and Haley Brenton turned to us.

She quickly introduced us and got right to the reason we were here. "The death of Gill Gross brings up a lot of questions. Is this related to the find of a treasure ship?"

I couldn't help but notice that the wall behind us had changed to a green screen. Images similar to what I had watched earlier were probably playing behind us.

Martinez answered. "It's too early to tell."

He went on in the boilerplate language that every law enforcement officer and politician uses when they don't know anything. Eventually the woman got tired of his "no comments" and turned her attention to me.

"Agent Hunter, you found Gross's body aboard his boat."

"Yes, the *Reale* was adrift inside the park. When

I boarded I found Gross already deceased." I thought I sounded like an idiot.

"Any sign of foul play?"

"It's an ongoing investigation." I felt the noose closing around my neck. She was good and let the silence hang, forcing me to answer. "We will issue information as it becomes available."

"So, you suspect foul play," she stated.

Martinez cleared his throat. "Agent Hunter is a seasoned investigator. We will issue a statement as soon as his investigation allows."

"I understand there was an autopsy last night. What was the result?"

"We need to notify the family first," Martinez said, dodging the question.

"So, you suspect foul play." Again, it was a statement. "Agent Hunter, what are the next steps in your investigation?" She looked directly at me.

"After I speak to his next of kin, there are some interviews I need to conduct."

"And I bet Vince Bugarra is going to be on the top of the list."

I had read about Bugarra in my brief internet search. He was one of Gross's competitors. "I'd rather not say."

Her nostrils flared and I could tell she smelled blood. "What about the electronics aboard? Surely there was a GPS."

"We have the unit and will make every attempt to recreate his last hours during our investigation," I said. From her smile I could tell she had gotten what she wanted.

"Thank you for your time, and we look forward to hearing more about this mystery," she said, dismissing us.

The lights dimmed and she said a quick thank you and good-bye before being hustled off the set. I turned to Martinez. The look on his face told me that I was in trouble.

Chapter 9

I couldn't get out of the building fast enough. It felt as if dominos were falling behind me and I didn't think I was going to stay ahead of them. Having a newscaster direct the investigation was not what I'd wanted. Martinez and I had a few words before I extracted myself and headed for the exit. I walked away feeling like I had been beaten, but also gained a new respect for Martinez—playing the media was harder than it looked.

Outside, I was surprised to see news vans and reporters from other networks. I wondered as I brushed away their microphones with a mumbled "no comment" what Martinez had received in return for the exclusive with this station.

I ran the gauntlet of the reporters, almost wishing I had waited for my boss to run interference.

He had been more forgiving than I had expected and reaffirmed that the case was mine. I knew he had ulterior motives, but I wasn't waiting around for the other shoe to drop.

Every other word I heard as I made my way to the truck was *treasure*. By the time the national networks ran the story this evening South Florida would be consumed by gold fever.

Two women stood by my truck. I could tell on first glance that they were related to each other and not with the media; their faces were nearly identical though their dress and demeanor were totally different. One of them, the older-looking of the two, approached. I was about to say that I had no comment and to watch the news when she held out her hand and introduced herself.

"I'm Gail Gross. This is Maria. Gill's daughter."

My Google search had revealed that he was divorced. I assumed this was his ex-wife. My assumption proved wrong.

"I'm his sister."

Box number one on my checklist was ticked. Gross's next of kin had appeared in front of me. I introduced myself and looked back over my shoulder at the crowd of reporters, camera operators, and sound people circling like a sailfish around a bait ball.

"Can we meet somewhere away from this? I'd like to talk to you."

"Sure, there's a coffee shop around the corner."

"I'll be a few minutes behind you. Might need a few evasive maneuvers to ditch this crowd." She smiled and the two women went to a richly appointed sedan parked across from my truck.

They were able to escape unmolested, but the paparazzi were descending on me. After fumbling to unlock it, I finally opened the door and slid inside. The truck came to life and I gunned the engine as a warning to the reporters, then cut the wheel hard to the right, away from the group. I sped out of the lot, hitting several speed bumps hard enough to smash my head into the overhead liner.

Once on the road, I remained vigilant, worried that a smarter reporter could have been covering the exits and then might follow me as a predator stalks its prey. After several quick turns, however, I felt comfortable that I wasn't being followed and pulled into a parking lot. Handing the attendant the ten-dollar fee, I asked if there was someplace I could park that would be out of sight. The park service truck was fairly nondescript, but it did have the tell-tale light bar on top. Another ten bought me a corner spot obstructed from the road. He took the bill and gave me a knowing look.

I left the truck, trying to remember evasive tactics from the spy books I had read. I circled the block once, looking at reflections in storefront windows that offered a view behind me. Finally, feeling foolish, I entered the coffee shop. The two women were already seated at a table, sipping their coffee. I decided to skip the line at the counter and sat across from them.

"Do you have any other information about Gill that wasn't released on the news?" Gail asked after she'd introduced me to Maria.

I studied her for a second. I knew her type and instantly classified her as Santa Cruz hippie. Probably a hardcore tree-hugging liberal, she was dressed in what might be construed by the casual observer as rags, but what I knew from my time in California were probably very expensive one-off designs Though she wore no makeup, her silver and turquoise jewelry completed her ensemble. "I'm assuming there is no current Mrs. Gross?" I asked if they could show me some ID; I had to make sure they were really the next of kin.

"I expect you'll be hearing from Jeanine, his ex, before too long. Piece of work, that one," Gail confided.

I noticed the cross look from Maria, who appeared to be her aunt's opposite. East Coast Elite described her well. Both her makeup and dress told me she was probably a diva. Her body language, as she looked down her nose that I suspect had been altered, confirmed my impression. Both women were blue-eyed and blond. The name *Maria* didn't quite fit the young woman in front of me. I wondered if it was in deference to the wrecks he'd sought. Nearly every Spanish galleon running gold back to the Continent had had *Maria* in her name. "It's really too early to tell you anything else. The autopsy revealed an embolism. We think he got it from ascending too fast."

"My dad was a careful diver. Who was the other diver on board?" Maria asked.

That was a new wrinkle I should have thought of already. The buddy system was taught like the gospel in scuba classes. *"Never dive alone"* as well as *"Don't surface faster than your own air bubbles"* were the two biggest rules I remembered from my training. Had Gross broken both? "There was no evidence of another diver. Do you know what he was working on?"

"He was always secretive about his projects. His backers were adamant about it. But if you find out…"

I added *backers* to my list of people to speak to. "Any idea who they were?"

"Only the IRS knows those names," Maria said.

She sounded bitter as if she had been excluded from something. "Did he have any enemies?"

They both snickered. "He was a treasure hunter," Gail said.

I guessed that implied enough. "Anyone specific?"

"These guys are worse than the long-dead European monarchs they are so obsessed with. One minute they're jumping in bed together; the next mortal enemies. I think every one of them has had it in for one another at some point."

There was something about the way she'd ended

the sentence that gave me the impression she had a name. I pulled out my pad and pen.

"There is one guy that I've never trusted," Gail went on. "Vince Bugarra."

That name kept popping up. "You know how I can find him?"

"You might ask Slipstream. He worked on and off for Gill."

I gave her a questioning look. "Does Slipstream have a real name?"

She returned my look with a shrug. "Anyway, I guess that's all we have. When do you expect the boat will be released?"

Interesting that she didn't ask about the body.

"Once the investigation is concluded," I answered and started to get up. My impression was that the Gross women were on a fishing expedition. They had offered up two names who could be their enemies—or competition.

Maria was fidgeting as if she had something to

say. I looked right at her. "Sorry for your loss," I told her. Her aunt started to rise and she followed. "Can I get your contact information?"

Gail gave me hers and started toward the door. I looked at Maria, who paused for a minute. "Just for the record." She looked down and recited her phone number.

"Do you know where he docked the boat?" I asked.

"Up the Miami River. Just before the airport there's a commercial marina."

I was pretty sure I knew which one she meant and let it go. They walked out of the coffee shop and I watched through the glass storefront as Gail turned to Maria. Their body language told me that they disagreed on something, but then they moved on, out of sight. I let them go before leaving the shop, and headed back to my truck. The brief conversation had at least yielded a few pieces of information, and I didn't expect a guy like Vince Bugarra would be hard to find. Identifying "Slipstream" and the location of the marina were my new top priorities. Hopefully I could find all my leads at the same place.

From the downtown location of the parking lot, I drove toward the river and followed it west. Over the course of a few miles the waterfront properties went from million-dollar condos to commercial buildings, then to industrial lots. I found the marina I thought was the one Maria had meant and pulled in. Hoping the woman in the office didn't remember me from my last visit, I left the truck next to the trailer where the office was located and knocked on the door.

I heard a voice call out over the rumble of the window air-conditioner vibrating in its frame next to the door. The command sounded enough like "enter" to give me permission so I opened the door and walked in. A blast of cold air hit me and the woman behind a single desk immediately motioned for me to shut the door. She looked like a flashback from the eighties, with spun-out hair and heavy makeup. I recognized her, but it didn't look like she remembered me.

"Hi, I'm Kurt Hunter with the National Park Service," I said, pulling out my credentials.

"I remember," she said with a heavy Russian accent.

That wasn't good. I had chased down a couple of thugs running women here and one of them might have been her boyfriend. "Gill Gross keep his boat here?" I asked.

"That's confidential. Got a warrant?" she sneered.

"We have his vessel already. I'm really looking for a guy that goes by the name 'Slipstream.'"

She made a huffing sound. "That no-good piece of crap. He's probably over by the roll-off, picking scrap metal out of it. Whoever gave him that name knew that one. Damned hard to get a day's work out of him. I'd be happy if you pulled him out of here."

Grateful for her change of attitude, I thanked her for the information and left the office.

Back outside on the steaming pavement, I decided that "marina" was a favorable description of the place. More of a parking lot circled by razor wire, the asphalt surface was cluttered with dry-docked boats in different states of disrepair or neglect. Off to the side I saw a long dumpster being used for construction debris and walked toward it.

As I approached, a coil of wire flew out, just missing me. "Slipstream?" A dirty face in the shadow of a bonnie hat appeared over the edge.

"Depends who's asking."

You had to be clever to come up with that one. I scanned the area for an escape route in case he decided to run and moved toward the only clear path. "Kurt Hunter, National Park Service."

"It's my brother poaching those gators. I'll swear on it."

His hands appeared on the edge and with a

move I didn't expect, he vaulted the side of the dumpster and took off toward the street. I went after him, but he was fast and knew where he was going. Just before he reached the road, I saw the office door open and the woman waddle out. She too was moving fast and once down the stairs she leaned over and grabbed a chain that lay across the entrance. Pulling it hard, it caught Slipstream just before he would have hit the sidewalk and disappeared.

"I'll forgive the last incident if you haul that piece of trash out of here," she said. Before I could answer she hustled back into the air-conditioned office.

Slipstream was down on the ground grabbing his ankle when I reached him. Rarely did I wear my gun belt, which had a supply of zip ties.. Looking down at the man, I figured I didn't need it anyway.

"I'll sue that bitch," he screamed in pain.

I reached down to help him up. Several inches shorter than my six feet, Slipstream looked rode hard and put up wet. I know the old cowboy expression applied to horses, but it fit here as well. It didn't take long, if you weren't careful, for the sun to take its toll on your appearance. Balding and wiry, he looked to be about sixty, but the stub of a cigar clenched in his jaw made him look older. I didn't need to frisk him; any object harder than a billfold would have been apparent against his skinny frame. "How about I take you to the emergency room and get that looked at?"

"Anything to get me away from Attila the Huntress."

He leaned against me, hobbling on his one good leg as we walked across the lot. I chanced a glance at the office when we passed and thought I saw the woman looking out the small barred window. Reaching the truck, I poured Slipstream into the passenger seat and went around to the driver's side.

"You ain't here about them gators, are you?"

"No, I'm looking into the death of Gill Gross. Heard you worked for him."

"Good damned riddance, if you ask me. And 'worked for him' ain't the way it was. We was partners, me and him. Anything we found we was supposed to split."

"And did he?"

"Between the damned state inspector and his daughter, I'm surprised he lasted as long as he did. Hounded him to death, they did." He realized what he'd said and looked down. "He was okay after they got their shares—until this last one, that is. Cut me right out of it."

I knew I was only getting one side of the story and the other side lay in the refrigerated case in the morgue. I had reached the entrance to the hospital and followed the signs to the emergency room. When we reached the entrance, I pulled off to the side and went around to help him.

"You know what he was working on?"

He dodged the question. "Hey, think you could use that title of yours to get me some painkillers?"

Chapter 10

I left a business card with the hospital administrator and headed back to the truck after an attendant helped him hobble to a wheelchair, then pushed him through the door for treatment.

When I reached the truck I checked my phone, saw a missed call, and hoped it was Justine with some kind of revelation that would make my job easier. The call was from Grace Herrera; probably returning my call from yesterday. It was unusual that she hadn't left a message.

The park service had little in the way of support for its law enforcement division. We had our boats, trucks, and radios, but that was about it. Miami-Dade and the Florida Department of Law Enforcement were our sources if we needed more. With the northern and western sides of the park adjoining Dade County, our cases tended to cross the imaginary borders, making working with them unavoidable. I had found it was often better to make a deal early and get their cooperation and use of their resources rather than wait until I needed them and get turned down. I sat in the truck with the windows open and returned her call. It went to voicemail, continuing our game of phone tag.

Vince Bugarra's name had come up too many times for me to ignore, but before I went after him I wanted more information. Slipstream had mentioned a state inspector. He hadn't called him out by name, but using the browser on my phone, I Googled a few terms and found the Florida Division of Historical Resources. After scrolling through several pages, I found a phone number for the Underwater Archeology Program. I dialed and waited. A woman answered. After identifying myself, I asked to speak to the chief. A minute later I had him on the line and explained who I was and why I was calling. "I need the name of your man in South Florida who worked with Gill Gross."

His attitude surprised me, though it shouldn't have. Bureaucrats spend their careers protecting their jobs and he seemed no different. I don't know whether it was because I worked for the federal government, but suspected it was standard procedure—information was not forthcoming.

"There is evidence of foul play and I have it on good authority that the inspector might have been one of the last people to see him alive," I explained. It was close to the truth, though calling Slipstream a "good authority" was a crime in itself. "You wouldn't want to interfere in a *criminal* investigation?" The threat didn't seem to affect him.

"Anything that involves what he was looking for or what he found *must* be reported to the department. Am I clear?"

I assured him that his turf was safe.

"Jim DeWitt," he finally told me. He recited the inspector's phone number and hung up before I could thank him. DeWitt's phone was probably ringing right now with orders to stonewall me. I dialed anyway, not surprised when the call went to voicemail.

I pulled out of the hospital parking and with no destination, I found a shade tree in a park that offered enough cover to turn off the air conditioning and open the windows. A city park service truck drove by and I saw its brake lights flash as the driver must have noticed the light bar on my truck and then the emblem. Not wanting another turf war, I backed out and left the park.

I remembered my conversation with Sid yesterday and decided to go see Vance at the Medical Examiner's office. There would be no need to continue the investigation if Vance ruled the death accidental.

On the way, I stopped at a convenience store for

a cup of coffee. I'm a black coffee guy, and would rather drink the motor oil served in gas stations than suffer the pretentious look of a barista when I order my coffee black. Leaving the truck, I entered the store and pressed a finger against each of the coffee thermoses, settling on a cup from the one that felt the most full.

At the counter, I took a sip from the styrofoam cup. I had to wait to pay while a heavyset woman dressed in a loose-fitting sweatshirt and pajama pants watched the attendant with a skeptical eye as he worked through the woman's pile of lotto tickets, checking each one under her watchful eye to see if there was a winner. I took another sip and stared blankly at the merchandise on the shelves behind the register: cigarettes, cell phones, rolling papers, and chewing tobacco occupied most of the space. My eyes went back to the cell phones.

Finally one of the tickets paid off, and the woman used the proceeds to buy more tickets and a pack of cigarettes. Moving to the side of the counter she gave me just enough room to set my coffee down while she sorted out her tickets. She had bought a handful of scratch-off tickets and started mumbling something to herself as she discarded the losers one at a time.

I did my best to ignore her and approached the clerk. "How much are the cell phones?" I asked.

He studied me carefully before answering, probably trying to evaluate which one to recommend.

"A smart phone would be good," I said, making his decision easier. If I was going off the reservation, I wanted to be all the way off and have my pictures and browser history private as well.

He turned and pointed to one. "This one is $79.95. I have a better one for twenty more—but you'll need a plan with it. Otherwise I have these that are pre-paid and don't need a credit card."

I ignored the burner phones. I was fine paying a hundred bucks and getting a real plan. "That's good,"

I said, taking the package and looking at the phone, noticing it was at least two generations behind the one in my pocket. I paid for it and the coffee and went back to the truck.

After fumbling with the packaging, I finally gave up and sliced through it with my knife. I found all the parts and plugged the charger into the truck's cigarette lighter outlet. There was a laminated paper with instructions to activate it. The phone had enough juice to start up, and leaving it plugged in I picked it up and entered my credit card information. A wave of guilt passed through me; I felt like I was doing something wrong—but that feeling didn't last long when the display lit up and showed my new phone number and five full bars of private unobservable service. Finally, the umbilical cord with Martinez was broken.

I entered Justine and Allie's numbers into the contacts and scrolled through my park service phone, looking for a number I hoped I still had. It had been more than a year since Mac Travis and I had worked together to stop a human smuggling ring. The well-orchestrated scheme, used old American car engines from the fifties, that were still common in Cuba, to power a fleet of salvaged fishing boats or *pangas*, as the locals called them. Once clear of Cuban waters, the refugees activated a stolen EPIRB that broadcast their position to the group. The smugglers would then use go-fast boats to pick them up. The *pangas* had then been recycled by a crooked cop that Justine and I had brought down.

After the smuggling ring's members had picked up each group of refugees, the men were killed and the women taken to sell. It was an absolutely evil, yet ingenious, plan that had worked until Mac and his sidekick Trufante found one of the boats in the Marquesas and I'd found another, floating with a dead body inside of the park. It had taken a team effort to bring them down.

I knew Mac to be reclusive. He lived on an

island off Big Pine Key, and it was a long shot to expect him to answer his phone. From what I remembered, if his phone was even with him it was rarely turned on. But he knew the salvage game and I needed help.

The phone rang twice before a woman answered. I was about to disconnect, thinking he had changed his number, when I remembered his girlfriend Mel. "Hey, this is Kurt Hunter. I'm looking for Mac."

"Me too. Let me know when you find him," she answered.

It appeared that Mac was still Mac. She wasn't being snarky and I continued. "I don't think we've met, but I'm with the National Park Service in Biscayne Bay. Mac and I worked together last year."

"Right, I remember. That deal with the EPIRBs."

It had been quite a bit more than that: Mel and Trufante's girlfriend Pamela had been taken by the men. "Any chance I can speak to him?"

"He's out with Trufante setting stone crab traps. They left at dawn. Unless Trufante finds some trouble, they're likely to be back any time."

I gave her my new super secret number and thanked her. Martinez didn't need to know about Mac. Setting the phones side by side on the seat next to me, I headed to the medical examiner's office.

It was an awkward necessity to carry both phones, but the freedom I now had to operate independently was worth it. With my park service phone in the front pocket of my cargo pants and my personal one in my back pocket, I left the truck and headed into the building.

Vance was working at his stand-up desk, drinking from a stainless steel tumbler that undoubtedly held some kind of concoction I had never heard of. He set the mug down when he saw me.

"I was just going to call you," he said, turning up

the ends of his mustache. "Been fishing again?"

I knew what he meant. "Nope, got this one paddling."

"What's the bite like?"

I gave him a rundown of the current state of fish affairs, noting that between training for the race and now this case, I hadn't been out in a few weeks.

Vance and Sid were as opposite as you could get. Probably a half dozen years younger than I am, Vance was all hipster. His haircut was straight out of the 1920s: long on top, shaved on the sides, and held back with a whole lot of product. His mustache was carefully groomed as well. Thankfully he had shaved his soul patch.

Coming from a guy wearing a too-tight untucked plaid shirt and skinny jeans that barely covered cartoon-patterned socks, it sounded like a different person was spouting the technical data that had come back with the tests.

I quickly got past the incongruence and focused

on what he was saying. The tox screen had come back negative—no surprise there. The news was that the brain scans showed that he had suffocated.

"There was no air left in his tanks," I said when Vance finished.

He thought for a second. "I'm not a diver, but we do get three or four diving fatalities here a year. Running out of air usually causes the victim to drown, not suffocate."

"What about the embolism?"

"It was still there, meaning he did ascend too quickly." He paused. "That and the fact that there was no water in the lungs led me to conclude that he was alive when he boarded the boat."

"So if he didn't run out of air, someone drained the tank to make it look like he had?"

"Possibly. And then killed him. You've got a murder on your hands."

I wanted to be sure of the sequence of events leading up to Gross's death, and combining our information, we came up with something plausible.

Gross had been diving, alone or not, I didn't know. He must have heard another boat above and expected foul play, which caused him to forget his ingrained safety procedures and bolt for the surface. When he reached the boat, someone was waiting for him and, already crippled by the embolism, he had been easy prey. The murderer had then cut the anchor line to allow the boat to drift off the site.

I thanked Vance and promised to take him out fishing soon, then headed out to the parking lot. Just as I pushed open the door, the phone in my back pocket vibrated. I jumped, not expecting it, and pulled the phone out. On the display was a number with a 305 area code. I recognized it right away.

Chapter 11

"Hey, Kurt. Mac Travis here."

"Hey, Mac. Got a case up here that I could use some advice on."

"Sure, go on."

I remembered him as being short on words and shorter on patience so I got right to the point. "You ever hear of a guy by the name of Gill Gross?"

"Sure, good and bad. From the folks I trust, mostly good, but I hear he may have hit a few bumps in the road lately."

Another reference to the treasure hunter having fallen on hard times, and coming from Mac I wasn't going to ignore it. I made a note to check his finances. "He died of what I would call, at this point, suspicious causes."

"Heard something about that through the coconut telegraph."

The Keys had their own under-the-radar network that was somehow faster than the internet. "I found the boat drifting in the park and his dead body was aboard."

"That's more your line of work than mine."

"There was evidence of some concretions on deck and my wife, Justine, found a whole object that we believe to be a silver artifact."

"Getting interesting."

I heard it in his voice—the treasure bug. "It appears that he was into some secret project. How would I figure out what he was working on?"

"His backers are likely to be tight-lipped. The state would know, but they're not very cooperative. You could pull your federal agent status on them."

"Left a message for the underwater archeologist." The line went silent. I was already surprised the conversation had lasted this long.

"Careful with how you deal with those guys. They have their own agendas, and it's not what I would call archaeology."

I wanted to know what he meant but could feel his patience waning. "Any other ideas? I checked his GPS and got nothing from it."

"Might have an SD card."

"The slot was empty. Just the numbers programmed into the unit itself."

"Doubt that'll help. Probably has some decoy spots on it. Anyone looking to move in on his find would know the GPS data on the boat would be worthless. Gotta be somewhere safe, maybe a handheld unit or on his computer at home where he can password protect that."

"I'll check into both those."

"Hey. Let me know how it goes." He paused. "I could run up there if you need a diver."

I thanked him and disconnected. His interest in the case surprised me, but I knew it was more from what Gross was working on than about finding his killer. He'd been helpful, though.

I hadn't thought to search Gross's house. I would need a warrant and that meant going through either Miami-Dade or Martinez. Grace hadn't returned my second call yet and I wondered if she was avoiding me. Anyway, things were moving along nicely without the locals' help, and I decided that as long as Martinez was being amicable I would use him. Somehow I often ended up needing warrants after hours or on the weekend. This was a Monday afternoon so it wouldn't require him to ask for any favors or use any capital. After a brief call and with the warrant being a sure thing, he agreed to help.

My next call was to Justine. It was before two and I caught her just getting out of the shower. Wishing I was there with her, I asked if she had found a handheld GPS or an SD card.

"Nope. Went through everything onboard. I didn't check his person, though; he was wearing a wetsuit."

That appeared to be a dead end. "I'm trying to get a search warrant for his house. Interested?"

"You bet. But, gotta have a case number or it's a no-go. You know, the *Kurt Hunter Rule*."

I remembered the new policy that we had jokingly named after me. In the past, I had used Miami-Dade's resources freely. They had put an end to that.

"I won't go over there until I talk to you first."

"Deal. I would like to follow through on the case. I'll let my boss know it's coming."

We signed off and I put the phone down. Looking at my new personal phone, I texted her from it.

A second later it binged. "Woohoo! Freedom!!" and a string of laughing emojis was her response.

When my work phone rang a second later and Martinez's name appeared on the screen, my first thought was that he had already cracked my new phone and was on to me.

"What the hell, Hunter?"

His greeting seemed to confirm that. "Got a call from Jackson Memorial. You know anything about a guy named Lucius Graves?"

"Slipstream?"

"What are you up to? They want to bill the Park Service for an examination, x-rays, and a walking boot. Who knows where it'll go from there?"

"He calls himself Gross's partner, but I'm guessing he's more of a helper."

"And that affects me or this department how?"

"He ran when I was trying to interview him. Tripped over something." There was no point telling him about the Russian woman. "I had to take him somewhere. I just left my name for the contact info."

"Yeah, about that. Don't be so freakin' naïve. This isn't small town California here. You're in Miami now, so start thinking like the low-life scum that you're dealing with."

The high he'd gotten from the TV appearance this morning had faded already. "I did get some useful information from him," I said.

"Good, because he's your new best friend and asked that you pick him up."

"Crap." I wasn't sure if I'd said that out loud. Martinez disconnected with another warning about being naïve. Still in the parking lot of the medical examiner's building, I looked over at Jackson Memorial and started the truck.

A few minutes of parking lot hopping later, I found Slipstream sitting on a bench by the entrance to the emergency room. He pushed himself off the bench to stand awkwardly on his new boot. Moving the heavy leg in front of him, he limped to the passenger side of the truck and opened the door. From the smile on his face, I guessed he had gotten what he'd asked for. The rattle of the pill bottle in his loose pants when he sat down confirmed it.

"Said it's just a sprain. Y'all lucked out, I guess."

There was no point arguing who was at fault here and Martinez had made it clear that I needed to pacify him enough to keep him from filing a complaint. Two could play at the not-being-naïve game.

"Where're we headed, boss?"

"Wherever you live." I had no need for a sidekick.

"Shoot, I got a stake in this, too. Ol' Gross done me out of some money. If we find anything I get my share, right? And screw that state dude."

He did know more about the treasure game than I did. If I could stand him, he might be helpful. "You better not hold anything out on me."

"Scout's honor," he said, holding up his right hand while his left hand fished the bottle of pain pills from his pocket.

I reached over and grabbed them before he could pop the lid. "No way. You work with me, you stay sober."

"Hey. Doctor's orders."

I doubted that and figured he had put on quite the performance to get the drugs. Looking at the label, I saw they were a blend of oxycontin and acetaminophen. Not the strongest pill in the medicine cabinet, but they could get him where he wanted to go—especially as I was sure he would increase the dosage by several times. I pocketed the drugs and looked at him.

"How do we find his backers?" Until the state underwater archeologist called back, they were next on my list.

"One I know is a big-time downtown lawyer. Comes out with us on weekends sometimes. Gross said there were a few more silent guys, but knowing him, he'd cap it at three."

"Why's that?" I asked, pulling out of the lot and heading toward downtown.

"How many bosses do you want?"

I could understand that. Back in the Plumas

Forest in California, I'd had one boss who was hours away. He left me on my own, asking only for incident reports and a vague schedule once a week. Now I had the king of the micromanagers sitting in his office watching me in real-time on his monitors. I placed a wager with myself about how long it would take him to find out I had a personal phone—not very long was my guess.

"Where's this guy at?"

"Top floor of a big ass building. Never been up there."

"What's his name?"

"Morehead something or other." He fished a fresh cigar out of his pocket, bit off the end, and stuck it in his mouth like he had done something to deserve it. My guess was that the hospital had surgically removed the last one and tossed it.

In one sense I got lucky, in another maybe not so much: I remembered the name of the firm I had written a five-figure check to during my custody dispute: Viscount and Morehead. It was hard to forget those luxurious offices and I wondered if I should call ahead, but figured we were close anyway, and if Morehead was in his office it would be harder for the receptionist to say no with me standing in front of her, rather than on the phone. Slipstream, of course, would stay in the truck.

We headed downtown. I found the building and parked in a loading zone right by the door. "If anyone comes by, just say I'll be a minute." I didn't expect trouble, but I was in Miami-Dade country.

"You let me look the dude straight in the face. I'll tell you if he's lying or not."

Slipstream was not going to be an asset in any way. He was staying in the truck. I tossed him a pill, which he grabbed like a pet monkey, in return for his compliance. Pocketing the container, I locked the truck and headed into the building.

Frantic is not the impression a high-priced law firm wants to give. That's usually a feeling reserved for the backrooms. But today even the plush carpet of the waiting room couldn't dampen the conversations going on behind the receptionist's desk.

"Mr. Hunter, are you here about Mr. Morehead?"

Her memory must have been the second attribute they had hired her for. The first was plain as day. I decided to play along and not show my ignorance. Asking what had happened to Mr. Morehead was probably a bad idea. "Yes."

"Come with me, please."

I came around the desk, walked through a heavy-looking door she opened for me, and followed her back to an office every bit as nice as Daniel J. Viscount's. I noticed this one had an opposite view; instead of South Beach, it looked out on downtown. Viscount came toward me.

"Glad you could help out," he said, shaking my hand.

"Sure." I still had no idea what was going on, but I was starting to expect the worst.

"Did Miami-Dade call you in?"

I let the question go, figuring he was going to keep talking—that's what lawyers do.

"No one has heard from Jake since Saturday afternoon. He was supposed to go out diving but never came back. His car has a locator on it. It's down in the Gables." He pulled out his phone and showed me a dot on a map. I knew the area, but the specific location meant nothing to me.

"Do you know anything about their relationship?"

"He was obsessed with Gross and this wreck. It was okay when he just went on the weekends, but he'd started taking time off during the week." He looked down. "Bad for billable hours."

I knew exactly what the hourly charge for their services was, and multiplied by eight hours each day it was a sizable figure. "It would be better to clear the room and let me have a look around." It sounded like he had already called Miami-Dade and the clock was ticking.

It was almost as liberating watching him follow my orders as it had been to make the first call on my new phone. Less than a minute later I found myself alone in Morehead's office. Viscount was the last one out and asked me to check in with him if I found anything.

Knowing my ruse could be exposed any second, I went directly to the missing attorney's desk. Hoping if I gave her enough notice she could finagle her way in here, I texted Justine to tell her about Morehead going missing and that Miami-Dade had already been called. I set the phone down and looked at the computer on his desktop. It was open to the home screen and I scanned the icons, not sure what I was looking for, but when I saw the compass rose icon for a GPS program, I clicked on it.

Chapter 12

The outer office was still a flurry of activity and I nervously waited for Miami-Dade to burst through the door and expose me, but I remained alone. I clicked on the GPS program and waited. There was nothing there except a screen to sync to his device. It did have one listed, though—that was a start if I could find it.

I knew I didn't have enough time to work my way through his computer. Instead I opened the Finder screen, hoping there would be a file he'd stored his waypoints in. Scanning the list I found the *.KLM* extension I was looking for and double-clicked it. An error message told me there was no program to display the contents of the file. Working back to the Finder screen, I found an Excel spreadsheet in his recently opened files that was labeled *Gross*. That had to be what I was looking for and I double-clicked again.

There was a commotion in the hallway and I expected the cavalry had arrived. I needed to get out of there quickly, but I wasn't going without the file. The spreadsheet opened; now I needed a way to download the data. A flash drive would be perfect. Pulling out the top drawers of the desk, I found nothing but promotional pens—not the plastic ones the rest of us got, but ones made of gold and silver. There was no flash drive and I looked back at the computer.

I heard distinct voices and knew my time was up. There was only one way to get the data—not the most efficient method, but it would work. Pulling out my phone, I took several pictures of the screen before pressing the power button on the back of the desktop unit. I hoped that would cover my tracks.

The voices were right outside the door and I quickly searched the room for the alternate exit I knew would be there. Daniel J. Viscount had one so I expected his partner would as well. There were two well-disguised doors on the wall to my left, both made to blend into the paneled walls. I guessed one would be a bathroom and the other an exit.

Door number one confirmed my theory, but it was the wrong one. I grabbed for the handle of the second door, opened it, and slid inside just as I caught sight of two detectives entering the room. It didn't matter where it led or what it was. I closed the door and waited until my eyes adjusted.

A single bare bulb lit a narrow hallway lined with roughly finished drywall that was just the fire tape used to satisfy the building code. It led to another door about fifty feet away and to the right. I walked down the corridor and checked the door. It was locked, and I had a brief moment of panic before I saw the deadbolt below the knob. Turning it released the lock, and after cracking it a hair, I saw it opened to the public hallway.

This corridor was empty and I left the cover of the secret hallway. Looking back, I could see it appeared to be just one in a line of panels. Unless you knew its exact location it didn't exist. I turned in the direction of the elevators, carefully staying against the wall. Two detectives had already entered the office, but with a high profile attorney missing I expected there would be more on the way. The last thing Miami-Dade wanted was to be sued by the firm for negligence.

I needed to cross in front of the elevators to reach the stairs. Though it was twenty flights down, the elevators would leave me too exposed. There was no telling who would be standing in the lobby when the doors opened. Just as I passed, I heard the familiar ping that the car had reached this floor and ducked into an alcove.

The elevator doors opened and I was surprised to see Justine. With an equipment case in each hand, she stood in the hallway looking at the placard across from the elevator doors that showed the directory of the residents' suites.

I waited until the doors closed behind her. "Hey," I whispered, moving out of the alcove slightly.

She jumped and looked around. I moved out another foot and she saw me.

"What are you doing here?" she asked, looking over her shoulder in the direction of the attorneys' office before moving toward me.

I pulled her into the alcove. "Got a tip that Morehead was Gross's main backer. Thought I'd pay him a visit."

"I thought that was your truck down there."

If she had seen it, the detectives probably had, too. I could only hope they were the norm for the department and not very good at detecting. "Can you let me know what you find?"

"Sure thing. Where are you going?"

"Have to get rid of Gross's sidekick."

She raised her brows.

"Long story. I'll call you in a bit."

"Might be here a while."

I kissed her and waited until I heard the door of the law offices close behind her before moving to the stairwell. Two at a time, I took the stairs to the main level. I was slightly out of breath when I cracked the door to the lobby. I should have asked Justine if any other officers were en route, but luckily the lobby was empty. Checking both directions first, I left the stairway and walked quickly to the exit.

Slipstream was leaning against the truck chewing on his cigar. His type seem to have an instinct for trouble and he must have sensed my urgency. He limped toward the passenger door and I barely waited until he'd hauled his immobilized leg into the cab before pulling onto the street.

After cruising through several yellow lights, I started to relax when a glance in the rearview mirror revealed that no one was following me. I looked over to check my phone, hoping for a return call from the state archeologist, but the screen was blank. Before I put it down, I flipped the setting from silent to vibrate and set it between my legs.

I had a moment of indecision, realizing that I had exhausted my leads. Gross's sister had been a dead end, clearly interested in what his estate would yield her, but that was about all. I suspected his daughter had more of an interest in her dad, but it was on her to call me. Martinez hadn't produced the warrant to search Gross's house and with Slipstream nodding off next to me and Morehead missing, my attention turned to the picture I had taken from Morehead's monitor.

My computer was at Adams Key, probably an hour and a half away judging from the sway of the palm trees beside the road. If they were moving like this inland, I expected the seas were running two to four feet. It would be a long, wet, bumpy ride out to the island and the action seemed to be here.

Looking over at my sleeping partner, I wondered if he had a computer. "Hey." I waited for a second and when there was no response I pushed his shoulder.

Slipstream jumped and looked around as if he wasn't sure where he was. I waited until he acclimated himself, thinking that I would have to space out his meds a little more. "You awake?"

"Just resting my eyes. In my line of work you learn to sleep with one eye open, you know."

He might not have been lying, because the cigar had not left its perch in his mouth. "Right." I stopped before the sarcastic comment on the tip of my tongue left my mouth. "You have a computer at home?"

"Yeah."

"Internet?"

"What do you think?"

"Think we could use it? I got some waypoints off Morehead's computer."

That perked him up and I wondered if it would be a mistake to let him see them. I had thought about going through the painfully tedious process of entering the numbers into my phone, but a computer would be much faster and a full-size monitor would give me the big picture.

"Like where Gross was when he was killed?" he asked.

"Won't know until we can plot them."

"I'm in," he said, giving me his address.

Slipstream lived in a two-story complex by the airport that looked like it had been built by the Army in the sixties. He directed me around back when he saw a heavyset man with a wife-beater shirt sitting in a lawn chair out front.

"Park over here." He directed me to an empty spot by the dumpster.

The lot was surprisingly full for a weekday afternoon, and I suspected that the day the welfare checks were delivered was a party around here.

Slipstream led me up the stairs to a door badly in need of paint. A window air conditioner was chugging along, spitting condensation on the walkway. I stepped around the puddle and passed an old set of aluminum jalousie windows that were cracked open, or more likely stuck in that position.

Slipstream pulled out a key, opened the door, and peered cautiously inside. He might have deemed it safe, but on entering I had to disagree. Partially empty food containers were scattered on the counters and an overflowing ashtray occupied the coffee table. Hoping that I would acclimate quickly, I started to breathe.

"Here you go." He moved to a small desk against a wall by the TV.

I took out my phone and sat in the chair. Slipstream hovered over me as I opened the photo app and found the best picture of the half dozen I had taken. He moved closer until he was almost touching me. Under a different set of circumstances I would have pushed him away, but even with the cigar he smelled better than the apartment.

After waiting for the screen to come to life, I spotted the icon for *Navionics*, a GPS program. I felt Slipstream move away as the screen opened and a map of the Miami offshore area opened. The first thing I noticed were dozens of pins, marking existing waypoints.

"Those are all mine," Slipstream said, moving farther away.

Fisherman, divers, and, I suspected, salvors guarded their numbers—they were their livelihood. From Slipstream's reaction, he had probably stolen them. Ignoring him, I started entering the coordinates in reverse order. My guess was that Morehead had added to the bottom of the list as he went rather than going through the trouble of adding rows to the top of the sheet.

It was tedious work, with Slipstream pacing behind me. Each waypoint was comprised of two numbers made up of nine digits each. After entering a set, I double-checked it against my photo. Several had typos, which I had to go back and correct. Slowly, after plotting the last five waypoints, a picture began to form. I heard a groan behind me at about the same time as I noticed that the points overlapped—all except for the last two.

The last number was closest to the park, but its location was still several miles from where I had found the drifting boat with Gross's body. Moving back from there, I could plot a path back to Government Cut, where he had probably started his days.

"Any of these look familiar?" I asked Slipstream. If he had them on his computer he had been there. "The last two are the ones I'm interested in," I said, hoping it would put him at ease. "I'm not judging."

He seemed to relax and took a position behind me. "First few are our old holes we checked several times. The last ones, though…" He paused. "Nope, don't recall ever being on 'em specifically. Lately we been spending a lot of time towing a magnetometer all over that area."

"Anything turn up?"

"Gross was secretive about that. He'd stay by the helm and have me work the deck. If he saw something he would mark it and check it later."

"Any idea what he was looking for?"

"Nope. He's always been a research guy. Most of the stuff he finds is because of all the studying he's done. Guy could even read the old-time Spanish. We wouldn't have been out there if he didn't know what he was looking for, but hell if he told me."

I wasn't sure if Slipstream was being truthful or not and for the moment didn't care as I zoomed into the last set of coordinates. Fortunately the Google satellite had shot the area on a clear day. The shallow reefs were visible, and the marker was placed right between one and what looked like a drop-off for the reef. The overlay was a NOAA chart showing exactly what the depths were. I had a good idea that this might be the perfect place for a wreck. Certainly something worth checking.

The outer reef, lying about five miles offshore, ran from the Marquesas, below Key West through Key Biscayne. Over the years hundreds if not thousands of ships had wandered or been driven onto the coral heads that lurked just below the surface.

"Ain't where I would have placed it, but Gill was a whole lot smarter than me."

He might have been a whole lot smarter, but his helper had stolen his numbers. Now, I had another one to watch.

Chapter 13

I would have preferred to go fishing. But, being newly married and staying in Miami, I decided to go with the flow, which meant a paddleboard workout with Justine. I should have bet her that she couldn't go a week without a paddle. Still disappointed with the DNF result of my first race, it took forever to warm up, and then I struggled with everything, especially getting my head into it. This was where fishing was different for me. The methodical effort of hunting and casting, especially with a fly rod, reached some inner part of my brain that solved things for me without my thinking about them. Watching Justine, just ahead of me, looking like she was effortlessly paddling into the rising sun, I felt she could enter the same flow state from paddling.

For me, staying upright and keeping up with her was all my brain could handle. I was still at the point where I had to think about every stroke; Justine had muscle memory for that built through the years and miles. Not that it was all bad; it just didn't solve my problems.

In the park, the water itself is spectacular but safe. Things changed above Key Biscayne, where the brilliant colors of the flats ended. Off the beaches of South Florida the water depth dropped quickly—to a hundred feet or more within a mile of the beach. Instead of the patch reefs of the bay, there were three distinct reef systems running parallel to the shore, the first as close as a hundred yards. The deeper water was darker and the currents swifter than the better protected bay, making it both dangerous and exciting.

I'd had enough and yelled over to Justine, "I'm going to check my phone." I carried my board above the high water mark. It took a few steps to regain my land legs and I went to where Justine's car was parked at one of the diagonal spaces running along A1A. Later on these would be packed, but this early in the morning the beach was quiet: walkers, shell collectors, metal detectors, a few fishermen wading in the surf, and us. This would not be the scene later, when boom boxes would break the stillness and the masses would cover every square inch of sand with colored blankets, umbrellas, and tents.

Usually we would load first, but I was hoping for a return call from Mac Travis and Justine was still on the water. I knew getting him on the phone was hit or miss and had left a message last night. After leaving Slipstream with two pills, enough to immobilize him and hopefully keep him out of trouble, I had left his apartment.

I had a dead body, a missing backer, and a handful of GPS numbers. Of those, the last two numbers were interesting. I had made sure to delete them from Slipstream's computer before leaving. It was those coordinates that I wanted to talk to Mac about.

My phone showed a missed call and a voicemail. Both the area code and number were unfamiliar. Leaning back against the hood of the car, I watched as Justine paddled out into the small breakers. She'd turn and watch the sets come in behind her then start to paddle, usually catching a small runner and a free ride to the beach where she would deftly spin the board just before it hit sand. It took a second for the voicemail to load and I held the phone to my ear.

Finally, the state archeologist had returned my call. He was available this morning between nine and ten. The message asked me to text back, letting him know where it would be convenient to meet. I looked at the display and saw it was already eight, barely enough time to get back, shower, and meet him. I pecked out a quick text confirming that I was available and left the name of a coffee shop around the corner from Justine's apartment.

Justine was coming out of the water, and

ignoring my fatigued muscles I quickly loaded both boards, strapped them to the rails on the car, and headed home. "The state guy finally called back," I told Justine to explain my rush.

"Cool, anything from Mac?"

"Not yet."

"You going to give him the thing we found?"

I didn't think I had any choice. It appeared to be a relic of some value. "I think I have to."

She must have sensed my dismay at losing the piece. Once the state had it we weren't getting it back, but if DeWitt found out that I hadn't disclosed it he could have my job.

"I'm almost done with the evidence and fingerprints from the boat. Maybe that'll turn something up."

I wasn't counting on it. The marine environment wiped evidence faster than Mr. Kaplan, the cleaner from *The Blacklist*. "Hope so."

"You hanging with your buddy again today?"

"Yeah, can't live with him; can't live without him." It was an odd pairing, but Slipstream was a person of interest, though I had nothing besides the potentially "liberated" GPS numbers on his computer. He would probably find trouble and possibly jeopardize the investigation if I let him out on his own.

She laughed. "I'll take Miami-Dade's finest for company over that creep."

We disagreed on that point, but it did steer my mind back to the missing attorney. He was tied to my case, possibly a witness to whatever had happened to Gross if he hadn't suffered the same fate. Gross was my case, but Morehead was Miami-Dade's. I could only hope the lead investigators would work with me. I made a mental note to call Grace again.

After a quick breakfast and a shower, I headed over to Slipstream's. It was close to nine, but the parking lot to the apartment complex was full to near-capacity. I left the truck and climbed the stairs to his unit. On the way up, I noticed several window shades move and doors crack open. The residents clearly had their law enforcement radar on.

It took several knocks before a bleary-eyed Slipstream opened the door. The cigar stub drooping from his mouth looked like it hadn't moved since I'd left him, and he appeared to have found something to supplement the pills I had given him. My watch told me there was not nearly enough time for me to make him presentable and still make my meeting with the state guy. All I could get from him was a vague promise that he would be ready in an hour.

It took pushing through several hard yellow lights, that I hoped didn't have red light cameras, to reach the coffee shop and I was still a few minutes late. A tall, lean man dressed in khakis and a short-sleeved shirt that said state employee all over it came toward the truck. I grabbed my phone and met him on the sidewalk.

"Jim DeWitt." The archeologist extended his

hand.

"Kurt Hunter." I never bought into the theory that you can tell a man's personality from the quality of his handshake, and I hoped I was right as I released the limp wrist. "Getting hot out here; come on inside."

He might have been a few inches taller, but I felt like I towered over him. I didn't run into too many academics, but his physical demeanor and patch of a goatee pegged him as one right away. His coffee drink seemed to match his personality: double macchiato, no milk, little foam. I stumbled over the words when I asked for it and was surprised when, added to my black coffee, the bill was over ten bucks. I asked for a receipt. Even if I had to get DeWitt to sign it, I was going to get Martinez to reimburse me for this.

We took our drinks to a corner table. With his eyes on the table, DeWitt fussed with his beard and stirred his coffee as if he were weighing the problems of the world. I guessed it was up to me to get the ball rolling.

"Did you work much with Gill Gross?"

"I don't know if *worked with* would be the right phrase." He continued to rub his beard, then took a sip of his drink. "I am the underwater archeologist in charge of this area. Lot of treasure hunters around," he said in a whiny voice, trying to sound like he was overworked. Slowly, he took another measured sip.

His pauses were getting annoying. "Can you tell me what he was working on?"

"He had several permits for different areas. Do you have the coordinates for where you found him?"

I got the feeling he was probing me for answers rather than the other way around. Pressing the home button on my phone, I was about to show him the picture I had taken of Morehead's computer screen but thought better of it. "The boat was drifting by the light near the Cape Florida Channel." I knew I wasn't being very specific.

"That's a fair ways from his closest permitted area."

We were getting nowhere. "Are the claims public record?"

"Yes, but they can be rather large areas and the state has a right to keep them private. Public safety, you know."

Or greed, I thought and decided to try a different tack. "What was the permit for? Anything brought up?"

That started the ritual all over: first the grooming of the beard, then the prolonged sip of coffee. "So, in a perfect world, we would have inspectors watching over every salvage vessel. Instead, with our limited budget, we rely on the prospectors to report finds. They generally stay within the boundaries of the law, but are very secretive. Are you sure you can't pinpoint where Gross was diving when he was killed?"

He certainly had a backward interest in this.

"Wouldn't the permits tell you? What was the closest?"

"Agent Hunter," he said, starting the beard thing again.

I didn't wait for him to start the coffee drinking ritual. I glanced at my phone screen, using it as an excuse. "I gotta go. Maybe if you think of something…" I handed him a card and stood.

He had continued anyway. Finishing his sip of coffee, he carefully wiped the foam from his mustache. "You have a responsibility to report any findings to my office." He countered with one of his own cards.

I left the meeting thankful that I hadn't brought the object sitting behind my seat in with me. I might have to turn it over, but he hadn't mentioned how quickly. After fifteen minutes with the bureaucrat, I found myself clearly sympathizing with the salvors. Looking at my watch, I figured Slipstream had had enough time to join the living. I left the parking lot and retraced the route to his apartment.

This time of year, the heat doesn't turn up until late morning, and I had decided to give the air-conditioning a break. That decision might have saved my life when I heard two men yelling at each other from the front of the apartment building. As I turned toward the back where Slipstream's apartment was, I noticed that the lawn chair previously occupied by the landlord was empty.

The argument seemed to pick up in intensity as I rounded the corner of the building. Slowing, I stopped when I saw the gun in Slipstream's wavering hand. He was leaning over the railing in front of his apartment pointing the barrel at the landlord, who was yelling back about the rent being late.

The landlord stepped back and reached behind his body. Thinking he was reaching for a gun, I slammed on the brakes and reached for my weapon before opening the door. Bracing myself against the door, I saw he was pulling out his phone. Slipstream was the only asset I had right now, and as flaky as he was, I couldn't afford for him to go to jail.

In the bright sunlight, the lights on my truck would be worthless and I wished I had a siren, or at least a hailer. Without either, I called out, "Drop the weapon and stand down."

I moved away from the truck, repeating the demand, twice more until I was in a position where Slipstream could see me. The landlord still held the phone, but it looked like he hadn't made the call yet. With my gun still pointed at the balcony, I moved toward him.

"Special Agent Hunter." I decided it was better to leave out the National Park Service part. "That man is a confidential informant."

"Him?" the man asked, looking up at Slipstream.

"What seems to be the problem?"

"The problem is the two hundred dollars he was short on the rent this month."

In many jurisdictions CIs were paid. I knew of

no precedent in the park service, but I needed him. Pulling my wallet out, I took out two hundred dollar bills and handed them to the man.

"And the twenty dollar late fee," he said, peering into my wallet.

I took out a twenty and handed it to him. "I'll need a receipt."

Chapter 14

The landlord gave me a smug look and walked away, leaving me staring up at the balcony. Now that Slipstream was on the payroll, I needed to figure out what to do with him. With the stub of the cigar looking like it was going to fall out of his mouth, he leaned over the railing and gave the landlord the finger. I thought about recommending that he apply to Miami-Dade; even without the cigar, he could stand in for Grace's new partner.

"Come on down, we have work to do," I called up to him. Slowly, I noticed doors closing and shades being drawn; the show was over. A few minutes later, with the stub still in his mouth and a fresh cigar sticking out of the pocket of his wrinkled shirt, he hobbled down the stairs.

"Damned leg is giving me fits this morning," he said as he dramatically set his reinforced leg on the sidewalk.

I knew he was fishing for a pill, but I wasn't buying.

"Not even going to thank me for paying your rent?"

"Shit, I could'a strung that old boy out till next month."

"Good to know." His skillset was impressive. "You know this DeWitt guy from the state?"

Before he could answer, a woman emerged from one of the first floor apartments and made a beeline toward us. She looked like the same woman who'd had the lottery tickets in the convenience store yesterday. My first thought was that I had somehow insulted her and she was after me, but when she reached us she smiled, showing a row of brown teeth.

"Your friend gonna pay me the gas money from last night?"

She must have seen my wallet. With her hands balled up in fists on her hips and one leg cocked forward, she was dug in.

"What's she talking about?"

"Damned taxi service is what I am. Now, you gonna pay me or what?" She reached for the cigar in his pocket.

He brushed her hand away and gave me that look.

"Twenty'll get rid of her and we can get to work," he said.

She moved closer to me and I could smell whatever she had been doing last night—and it wasn't good. It was worth the twenty to get rid of her. After I'd fished the bill out of my wallet, she snatched it and it disappeared into her shirt.

"Anytime, boys," she said, and walked away.

"You go somewhere last night?"

"Nah, she's just crazy is all."

I could believe that, but I didn't believe him. I

had seen how meticulously she handled her lottery tickets. She didn't miss details.

Slipstream changed the subject before I could ask again. "You were wanting to know about DeWitt? Yeah, I know him."

We agreed on something. "How's he work?"

"What do you mean?"

I started walking to the truck, not wanting to be overheard by the neighbors, some of whom were still watching. I waited for him to haul his stiff leg over the curb to the parking lot. "Is he on the water? In an office? How does he find out what's going on?"

"Whoa there. That's a lot of asking."

"By my account it about covers the late fee I just paid for you. We haven't got to the gas yet. Then there's still going to be the matter of the rent." We had reached the truck and he waited for me to unlock his door. "Look. I've taken care of your foot and rent. Anything else I can do for you or are you going to cooperate? I thought Gross was your friend."

"Partner."

"Whatever." We hadn't even left the parking lot and he was already on my last nerve. I thought for a second about pairing him with Susan McLeash. That put a smile on my face. Finally, I unlocked his door and he climbed in.

"Where we goin'? I could use some breakfast."

That wasn't going to happen. "That state guy sounds like he's playing both sides. You know where to find him?"

"Any bar he can find."

I was getting used to his quippy answers, but it still bothered me. "Any one in particular?"

"Over by the Miami Beach Marina there's a place loaded with his type. Couple of others up the Intracoastal, too."

I knew the marina and bar all too well and made a note to pay a visit to my buddy Gordy from Bottoms Up Boat Cleaning. Slipstream was definitely on the mark, putting those two in the same boat or bar as it were.

It was getting close to noon, but still a little early for the bar crowd. I'd found that hardcore drinkers drank at home during the day, waiting for the reduced prices of happy hour before heading out. With a few hours to kill, I wondered about the object sitting behind the seat. It might answer some questions if I knew what it was. Before I could figure that out, the phone rang. I tried to hide my smile when I saw it was Justine.

"Hey."

"Hey back. I got called in early to process Gross's house. Interested?"

"For sure," I answered, wondering why Martinez hadn't let me know the warrant had been issued. She texted me the address and we agreed to meet in forty minutes. I disconnected the call and pressed the text. The map app opened and routed me to a neighborhood in Coral Gables. The ETA was thirty minutes, which gave me a little time to ditch my partner. After seeing the GPS waypoints on his computer, there was no way I was letting him in that house.

"You gonna feed me or what? Can't be working on an empty stomach."

It was actually a good idea. "Sure. Got some business in the Gables, I'll drop you somewhere there." I wondered if he ate with the cigar stub in his mouth.

That seemed to satisfy him for now. I expected he would be asking for a pill afterward, but I would cross that bridge when I got there. Following the directions on my phone, I followed 836 until the I-95 exit and headed south. A few blocks before the turn off South Dixie Highway came up, I saw a small Cuban restaurant in a strip mall.

"Cuban okay?"

"You're buying."

I handed him a twenty, asked for a receipt, and was glad when I had the truck back to myself—but his presence still lingered. He only chewed the cigar, but it took the combination of the open windows and air-conditioning to evacuate the smell.

The GPS directions had me turn into a neighborhood of older ranch homes. Reaching Gross's house, I saw a red Jeep Wrangler in the driveway. Passing the house, I took a spin around the block, both to kill time until Justine got here and wanting to get a feel for the neighborhood. It was always a good idea, especially in the older areas, to make sure there weren't neighbors with a dozen Harleys or muscle cars out front.

Most houses appeared to be well maintained, but looked vacant. Only a few had cars in the driveway. Quite the opposite of Slipstream's apartment complex; most of the residents here appeared to be at work. Finally pulling up to the curb, I stared at the house for a second. I had Gross for a pickup guy, not a red Jeep guy. I removed my gun belt from the glove compartment and buckled it around my waist as I approached the house.

The front of the house faced east and had tinted windows to keep out the morning sun. They were as effective at concealing the interior as they were at keeping out the heat. Moving toward the door, I looked for a doorbell and not finding one, knocked with the butt of my gun. I could have waited for Justine. She would have the paperwork to gain entry legally, but if someone answered, as I expected they would, I was going in now.

"Who is it?" A young woman's voice came through the wooden door.

My feeling was correct. It sounded like Gross's daughter. "Agent Hunter. I have some questions."

The door opened part way, stopped by a chain. The same emerald eyes that I had seen in the coffee shop peered out at me from the dark interior. The door closed and then opened.

"Come in," Maria said, opening the door all the way.

This was definitely a man's house: neat rather than clean. The counters and tables were bare and it looked like everything had its place—everything except for the boxes in the middle of the living room. There were about a half-dozen already full and sealed and another dozen or so in the process of being packed. My first instinct was to stop her, but this wasn't a crime scene and she was Gross's daughter. I doubted it, but there was also the possibility that she lived here. If not, the house had probably been bequeathed to her.

"We've got some forensics people on the way," I said, wanting it to sound more like standard procedure than a question.

"Sure. I'm just packing some family things. I guess I'll put the house up for sale."

I wondered how a famous treasure hunter's house would be priced. There had to be people out there who'd think there was buried treasure here. "Good market."

"Hope so."

I remembered the feeling that she'd been holding something back in front of her aunt. There might never be a better time to see what that was. "Your aunt seemed a little bitter."

"My dad worked his butt off for everything he had; she's different. Always wants something for nothing. She expected him to take care of her."

"Thought she said she was divorced."

"Twice, but she's burned through whatever she got long ago."

"Are you worried she'll go after the estate?"

"You call this an estate? Dad worked hard, but he was always chasing rainbows and that gets expensive. He could easily lose more searching for a wreck that he never found than he' d make on one he did. And then the state had to take their cut."

"Did you have much to do with his business?"

"I helped with his books and taxes. Stuff that wouldn't get done otherwise."

"What about the state inspector?"

"Yeah, Dad couldn't be in the same room with that guy. I dealt with him."

Finally, a break, but just as I was going to ask to see the records the crime scene van pulled up. "DeWitt, right. I got the same feeling about him." When I heard my own words, I knew I had better watch myself. I remembered Martinez's comment about being naïve. The human race was more devious than I gave it credit for. Making judgments based on instinct about the people involved in a case had gotten me in trouble before.

A knock on the door interrupted us. Maria went to open it and when Justine entered, I made the introductions.

"Maria Gross, this is Justine Doezynski, from the Miami-Dade lab." We hadn't worked out Justine's last name status yet. She was happy to lose the Doey nickname, but we often ended up working together and one Hunter in the room was usually enough.

"Hey. Sorry about your loss," Justine said, setting her cases down. "Mind if I have a look around? If there is an office, that would be a good place to start."

"Sure, last door at the end of the hall," Maria said.

Justine picked up her cases and left us alone again. I looked around the room, waiting until Justine was out of earshot. There was nothing I wanted to hide from her, but I did it for Maria. While I waited, I walked over to the floor-to-ceiling bookcases that took up one entire wall. There were two sides to everyone; what they showed the world, and what they hid. I was hoping that the contents of the bookshelves would tell me a little about the man, but I also knew that finding out what was on his private bookshelves was more important.

"Do you have any paperwork or correspondence with the state?" I asked, as I scanned the shelves. They didn't hold any actual artifacts, but there were plenty of pictures and books. Every second or third spot had something missing, which I guessed was in the boxes on the floor. "He find all these?"

She nodded. Before she answered about the paperwork, Justine called out.

"Hey, there's someone in the backyard by the shed."

Maria followed me to the office. Justine stood in front of a pair of french doors that led to a small patio and walkway. At the end of the walkway was a detached garage. A man was hunched over by the door—Jim DeWitt.

Maria was through the patio door before I could stop her. Not knowing DeWitt's intentions, and assuming from her actions that he was not invited, I pulled my weapon and followed her.

"What are you doing? I asked you to stay out of there." Maria screamed at him.

He turned and quickly put something in his pocket, then held out his empty hands. "Just looking to recover what belongs to the State of Florida."

"He paid you twice over," Maria yelled. "I told you we would reconcile all of that in due time."

DeWitt saw me standing behind her. He appeared to be no threat and I put the gun away.

"Agent Hunter. Perhaps as a federal agent, you can tell Ms. Gross here that the state gets paid first."

"I would think a probate judge would decide that."

"An inventory would be suitable for now," DeWitt said.

Something was going on between the two of them and I had the feeling I was being asked to referee.

She gave him a nasty look. "There are things in process in there that aren't to be disturbed." She turned to me. "I'll get the key."

A minute later we were standing in front of the door. DeWitt, happy that he was apparently getting what he wanted, gave Maria enough space that she couldn't reach him. We were all curious in our own ways about what was inside and when Maria opened the door, we all jumped back as one.

Chapter 15

For the second time in almost as many days, I smelled death before I saw it. We jumped back in order of our experience: Justine was hardly affected; I gagged, but tried to remain stoic and held my ground; DeWitt took several steps back; and Maria screamed.

Justine gave me a look that told me to get rid of her, and I escorted her back to the house. When I returned, DeWitt seemed glued to his spot. I didn't want him around Maria or otherwise in the way and figured that was good enough for now.

"I have to call Miami-Dade," Justine said, pulling her phone from her pocket.

There was no choice. Gross was mine, but Coral Gables was not in my jurisdiction. "Can you at least call Grace?" I would have to work closely with whomever the case was assigned to; at least she was an ally. Justine stood pensive for a second, as if I had somehow insulted her, and considered my request. There was some kind of bad blood between the two women and if I was going to stay sane, I needed to find out what it was. Though both were professional, but just under the surface, something always seemed to be percolating between them,.

"I have to call dispatch. There're procedures."

"What if I call?" I wasn't burdened by the massive rules and regulations of the county—only Martinez. That wasn't always better, but in this case, he'd be happy enough I had called anyone besides him.

"Suit yourself, but if she doesn't answer…"

"Okay." I stepped to the side and found Grace's number in my contact list. It wasn't like the success of my search for Gross's killer was on the line whether she answered or not, but it would be affected.

"Agent Hunter."

I breathed an inaudible sigh of relief. "You working?"

"You know it. "

From what I had seen of the department, she had one of the better work ethics, though I still didn't know why she had not been returning my calls the last two days. "Got a body in the Gables."

"Related to your case?"

"Found it in the garage at Gross's house. Justine is going in to have a look."

"Tell her to wait and give me an address and I'll head over." She disconnected, and I texted her the location.

I failed to relay the message and watched Justine put on gloves and remove a large mag light from one of her boxes. She handed me a pair of disposable booties, which we both put over our shoes before entering. My case or not, I had no intention of waiting for Miami-Dade to have a look at what was inside.

Together we crossed the threshold. Justine flicked on the light switch and suddenly the dark garage was transformed into a laboratory from a *Breaking Bad* episode. Stainless steel tables sat on an epoxy-coated floor. The drywall was covered with a plastic-looking finish and the lighting was about twice what you would expect from a garage.

The next thing I saw was a pair of very expensive shoes. Standing back to allow Justine to do her thing, I followed in her footsteps. My eyes moved from the body to the shiny objects soaking in bins on one of the tables. There seemed to be a progression the closer I got to the body. The contents of the closest bin were black concretions similar to the chunk we had found aboard Gross's boat. As I moved closer to the body, I could see the concretions were gone, revealing artifacts in their natural state. The last bin was overturned. Shiny silver objects, mixed in with a good deal of blood, were scattered on the floor. Even my uneducated eye could tell these were not from Spain's glory days. These looked new, but not twentieth-century new; maybe from the eighteen hundreds. Justine cleared her throat and brought my attention back to the body. Looking up from the shoes, I scanned him until, moving around a large container, I saw the head wound that had killed the man. The blow had been to the back of the skull, as if he'd been approached from behind. Moving to the side I saw the face was intact. There was no doubt we had found Morehead.

Justine tossed me a pair of gloves. One landed in my hand, the other dropped to the ground. I leaned over to pick it up and glanced back through the doorway. DeWitt had disappeared. I hoped he hadn't gone in to confront Maria.

"DeWitt is gone. I'm going to have a look around."

"I got this," Justine replied.

I knew her well enough to not take her

abruptness personally. Of all the techs I had seen since coming here, she was the most thorough and part of that was her focus when she worked alone.

With my distrust for the state inspector pegged into the red zone on my alert scale, I crossed the path to the house. Knocking on the doorjamb, I entered through the kitchen door. "Maria," I called out. There was no answer, and I waited several seconds before moving into the kitchen. Louder this time, I called her name again. When I received no answer I drew my weapon and started searching the house. From my view out the living room window, I could see the Jeep was gone.

Moving back through the rooms I retraced my steps, hoping not to disturb any evidence. I left the house went back to the garage. "Maria's gone, too."

Justine appeared in the doorway holding a wallet. "I think we found your attorney."

We were on the walkway outside the garage and both turned to the street when we heard a car pull up. Coming in a little too hot, its passenger side wheel slammed into the curb before the driver straightened it out.

"That was quick," Justine said.

Grace got out of the passenger seat and brushed herself off. She said something to the driver that I couldn't make out and walked over to us without waiting for her partner.

John Traynor, or JT as he preferred, stepped out of the driver's side and slammed the door like the equipment and not the operator had caused the car to hit the curb. He went around and kicked the wheel before joining us.

Grace had bad partner karma. Traynor's predecessor had been a piece of work as well. Abrasive, sarcastic, and lazy, he was a perfect fit for the department, and had even been promoted for it.

"You need to wait until we establish a perimeter and the coroner gets here," Grace said to Justine. "You of all people know the procedure."

Justine stood with the wallet in her hand. Her jaw dropped and a look of indecision covered her face. I could see the gears turning in her head, having the inner debate about whether to confront Grace. Although she was my wife, I had no idea what the department protocol was, and feeling helpless and guilty for not being able to come to her aid, I stepped back and let her decide how to handle this.

To make matters worse, Traynor stepped between the women and reached for the wallet. His courage surprised me, but standing less than five-six, he was able to move in under the taller women's gazes.

"Step in some more shit, Hunter?" he asked.

"John. Good to see you too." There was no way I was giving him the satisfaction of calling him by the initials he preferred. Even his last name was too cool for the detective.

"We'll need your statement," he said.

I decided with the air buzzing with estrogen

from Justine and Grace that it wouldn't be a good idea to add testosterone to the mix. "We may have a missing suspect as well." They all turned to me.

"Gross's daughter Maria was here when I arrived. Just after Justine arrived to process his office, we saw a man trying to break into the garage. That's how we found the body." The next part was hard to say. "He disappeared in the confusion and when I checked the house Maria was gone as well."

"Maybe she couldn't stomach all this?" Grace said.

"Or she knew what was in there." Maybe Maria had put on a carefully crafted facade of the grieving daughter; it could all too easily be an act.

"Okay. Let me have their details and I'll call in a BOLO for both of them," Grace said.

I gave her the names and descriptions and we waited while she radioed the station. "This whole property is a crime scene," she said to Traynor. "Tape it all off and start a log of who goes in and out."

Her orders had the same effect as a slap in the face, but he was the junior officer and went to the car, opened the trunk, and took out a jumbo-sized roll of crime scene tape.

Justine and I moved to stand under a shade tree outside the perimeter of the crime scene Traynor had established himself inside, waiting with a clipboard to log in anyone who entered.

"What's the deal?" I asked Justine.

"They're just following protocol."

"I mean between the two of you."

"Nothing."

There are only two options when a woman says "nothing." I chose the safer one and didn't pry. She understood the layers of the Miami-Dade bureaucracy better than I did. "What's Traynor's deal?" I asked.

She shrugged. "I think he resents being partnered with Grace."

I wondered if it shouldn't be the other way around. "Any dirt on him?"

Grace came towards us. She must have heard the last part of our exchange. "He's just brash and arrogant; fits right in here." She paused. "Hey, sorry about not returning your calls. Every time it rings, he's breathing down my back like it's his business. We've had a busy few days."

The brakes squealing on an approaching van cut short our conversation and we both turned to the sound. The medical examiner's van came barreling down the street with Sid hunched over at the wheel. It screeched to a stop only inches from the cruiser that Grace and Traynor had arrived in. We both went toward the van to help.

"You need to go back to fishing, Hunter. You didn't catch nearly this many when you were on the water," Sid said as he climbed out of the van and stretched his back.

My reputation as a shit magnet was intact. "Wish

I could," I told him and helped him unload a gurney.

"I guess if you stopped finding bodies, my girl here would get bored with you. What do we have here?" he asked.

"One of Gross's backers. I had a quick look before Herrera and her new boy toy tossed me out. Looks like he was hit in the back of the head."

"Let's go have a look, shall we?" He put his arm around Justine's shoulders and lifted the yellow tape. Traynor stuck a clipboard in Sid's face, which he calmly pushed away. Several other official cars pulled up and the scene was soon crawling with officers. Most ignored me and I realized there was nothing else I could do here.

Heading back to the truck, I texted Justine that I was going to try and find Maria and DeWitt. I had no problem leaving the deceased to Grace and Traynor; the case was going to be solved by finding the living.

My phone revealed several messages from Slipstream. Apparently he'd finished breakfast and was ready for action. In truth I guessed he wanted me more for the pills than anything, but he knew these guys and how they rolled. I texted him back that I was on my way and headed to where I had dropped him off.

Pacing the sidewalk in his walking boot, he seemed anxious when I pulled up. "Where have you been?" he asked between bites of his cigar.

There was no point in withholding anything from him and hopefully letting him tag along with me would not only help my investigation, but now that Morehead had been found dead, keep him alive. He looked at me with his bloodshot eyes. I caved in and fished his pills out of my pocket, opened the bottle, and handed him one. In less than a second it was gone.

"We have to find DeWitt."

"Now that's a pair for you."

"They know each other?"

"Gross wouldn't deal with DeWitt. Maria

handled him, if you know what I mean." He gave me a Groucho Marx nod with his cigar.

"What about Gross's sister?" Of the cast of characters still living, she was unaccounted for as well. "She seemed a little bitter when I met her."

"Bitter ain't half of her. That be one entitled bitch. Harmless, though." He spat out a piece of the cigar. "She makes her living by getting married, not widowed. A string of dead husbands is bad for business."

"If you were DeWitt, where would you go?"

"Pawn shop most likely."

I got his meaning, but he didn't know that DeWitt hadn't gotten inside the garage. I moved on the Maria. "The only car there was a red Jeep."

"That'd be Maria's ride. DeWitt has a state car, you know, white SUV. Wonder how he got there."

He was smarter than he looked. "I didn't see it near the house." I was confident my federal employee radar would have spotted it.

"Sneaky bastard, that one."

DeWitt was involved in this. I wasn't sure if he was protecting the state's interest or lining his pockets—maybe both, but I knew I had to find him.

Chapter 16

If I had learned anything from Martinez, it was that every government asset was tracked. With Slipstream under the influence of the pill I had given him and snoring quietly in the passenger seat, this was my best opportunity to find DeWitt. I glanced over at my new partner, wondering if I should rescue the cigar that was held in place by a small pool of saliva on his bottom lip. That would probably be the easiest decision of the day. I left it there and turned my attention to finding DeWitt and Maria.

The BOLO had been out for over an hour now; checking in with Grace told me there'd been no responses. Martinez might not know about the BOLO, but there was no point hiding it from him. He might also be happy to know that Miami-Dade was now involved, which would ease his budget woes and mitigate the fallout if I failed.

Mariposa answered, and after a few minutes of small talk and the promise of another dinner she connected me to the boss. I was thinking about her husband's guest-only Appleton 21 rum when Martinez picked up.

"Well, this is a surprise. Special Agent Hunter calling me. To what do I owe the honor?"

From his sarcasm, I guessed that Susan McLeash was sitting there. "Jim DeWitt; he's an underwater archeologist working for the state."

"What about him?"

"He disappeared from a crime scene. Also, we've got another body. We found Morehead in Gross's garage."

"I heard there was a BOLO out for DeWitt. What does this have to do with the park?"

This was where it was going to get tricky. In his world, favors were a kind of bureaucratic currency and he would be loath to spend any capital if Miami-Dade could get the same result. "DeWitt is a person of interest in Gross's murder."

"That accusation better have some substance behind it."

Along with granting favors, protecting each other was also in the bureaucrats' manual. The ice was getting thinner with Martinez looking after his brethren. "It's complicated, but I believe he may be in cahoots with the family."

"Maybe we should be having this conversation face to face. I want to be sure you can read my lips when I tell you to back off."

I was being summoned and all I could hope for was that I could talk him into helping in person. Susan McLeash, as usual, might be the key. Although she was often forced on me and was a wild card in any situation, I had finally figured out what her skillset was. Even though it was dangerous, I'd had some success using her. "Okay, I'll be there in thirty minutes." I paused, looking over at Slipstream. "I also have a confidential informant that I'm bringing in."

The line went dead and I pulled out of the parking lot. Traffic was starting to pick up as the early exodus from Miami had begun. Slipstream was jolted awake by a bone-jarring pothole, but quickly fell back to sleep. I couldn't help but look over at him. The cigar had survived and I started to make a bet with myself about what it would take to actually jar it loose. While I navigated my way to the turnpike, I tried to think of the best way to use my new secret weapon. If two negatives could equal a positive in math, teaming him up with Susan McLeash might be an option worth pursuing.

After pulling into an open space behind the headquarters building, I poked him in the ribs. The cigar jiggled and I thought for a brief second he was going to lose it, but he woke up and saved it.

"Wait here," I told him as I exited the truck.

He gave me another look, like he wanted another pill, but I needed him conscious for now.

"Where are we?"

"Homestead, behind the park service headquarters building."

"What the hell are we doing here?"

"I have to report to my boss. Justify all the expenses that you're running up."

"Shoot, the feds don't care."

If he only knew my boss. With only a few years to go until retirement, Martinez was doing anything he could to get a promotion and increase his pension. That included one of the favorite games of the bureaucrat—spend your entire budget to the penny, but don't exceed it. That insured that next year's allocation would remain the same and he wouldn't be accused of running an inefficient department. If private businesses were run like this, the bankruptcy courts would be standing room only.

"Just wait here. I'll come get you in a few

minutes." I locked the truck, hoping that in his current condition that might keep him there. Mariposa greeted me with her usual warm smile and gave me a heads-up on the mood upstairs. I thanked her and headed to Martinez's office.

As usual, he feigned being on an important call and waved me to the open seat, which was carefully situated in order to obscure the screens of the three monitors on his desk. The other seat was usually reserved for Susan McLeash, and I was surprised to find it empty.

"Well?"

I almost replied with a *well what*, but held my tongue, thinking he would continue on his own.

"Have you gotten anywhere with finding Gross's killer or are we just watching the body count add up?"

I wasn't sure where this was going. "Miami-Dade has the last one. It's in their jurisdiction."

"I heard from their chief earlier. It seems they're

trying to take Gross's murder off your plate as well. I don't have to tell you that solving this case would be huge for the park—especially if what he was working on was inside our waters."

So he wasn't telling me to back off after all. There it was. Everyone wanted a piece of this case for different reasons. Martinez wasn't in it for the riches, just for the exposure and his budget. We had added an artificial reef made from the rubble of the collapsed FIU bridge a few months ago. The eighteen mooring balls that Ray and I had secured to the site were constantly full. Adding a legitimate wreck, like a treasure ship, would be a huge boon for the park.

"I need some help penetrating the Florida Division of Historic Resources." Asking him for help hurt and I knew from his expression that he knew it. He folded his hands under his chin. At least I had his attention. "Jim DeWitt, the state archeologist, has to have known what he was working on. There are permits for everything."

"You say that like it's a bad thing."

I was not going to debate my feelings about government intervention with him, or reveal the GPS numbers I had. "With DeWitt on the run, we should be able to access those records." I wasn't sure that we could, but we were a federal agency and DeWitt worked for the state. There had to be some power in that.

"If I were the special agent on this case, I would find DeWitt before causing trouble in Tallahassee," Martinez advised.

I had half-expected him to backtrack and cover for DeWitt. It wasn't my "A" plan, but he'd fallen into my trap. "Can we track his SUV?"

"Just like that? You think I can hack into the state system?"

I knew he could, but he would need to come to it on his own. "What is Susan up to?" I asked.

"Just took some vacation time. I was thinking about assigning her to help you. This is a high profile case and I'm not happy with where this investigation is going."

If there was a way to get to him it was through involving my nemesis. But, if I could manage her, I would have his full support. "My CI is downstairs. I'm thinking she could work with him. He knows where these guys all hang out." A little reconnaissance wouldn't hurt and if there were bars involved, Susan would be all in.

"Good idea. I'll have her contact you."

I didn't want to ask where she was. I'd passed her empty office on my way to his, and looking out his window I could see her boat tied up, ready for a hurricane. The lines from my own boat, which hadn't been out since last week, were still looped over hers, telling me that hers hadn't been out in a while. "So, about DeWitt?"

"Give me a little time. I know some people with the state who might be able to help. Just make sure this isn't a wild goose chase."

I sensed I'd been dismissed and quickly exited his office. Before I was out the door, he had already started pecking on his keyboard, making a show of responding to some urgent email demanding his immediate attention.

On my way out, I stopped by Mariposa's desk. She was packing up her things to go home and I realized how late it was. Hopefully Martinez would follow through on DeWitt before he left. "Have you seen Susan?"

"Funny, you asking for her," she said in her sing-song accent and laughed.

"I have the perfect job for her," I said and winked.

"She left about an hour ago. Looked like she was upset, but that's a usual state of affairs for her."

That was our mercurial Susan McLeash. "Well, you have a good night and say hello to your husband."

"And the same to you. How's that girl of

yours?"

"All good. Hopefully she'll be down this weekend." I thought about Allie visiting in a few days and hoped the case was wrapped up by then. Leaving the building, I turned toward the back lot and started for the truck. I was only halfway across the parking lot when I saw the passenger seat was empty. I closed the fifty feet to the truck in a half-dozen hurried strides. Basing my plan on Slipstream and Susan McLeash hadn't been the brightest idea, but it was the only one I had—and now both of them were missing.

Slipstream couldn't have gone far with only one good leg and no vehicle. I started searching along the mangrove-lined bank of the canal behind the building. There was no sign of him there and I continued on the walkway that ran alongside the water. The farther I moved away from the truck, the faster I went. Passing the view of the Miami skyline across the bay, I continued to a small point by the visitor's center with its meeting rooms, small museum, and gift shop. I glanced up, but saw no sign of him. But then around the corner, standing on a thin strip that was more mud than sand, I found him gazing out at the water.

"You know how many wrecks are out there that haven't been found? Tons of gold and silver sitting there for the few willing to take the risks and find it."

I let him go on, sensing there was something he was trying to say.

"It's the people like Gross, and even the backers like Morehead, that make it happen. Did you know that Mel Fisher spent seven million dollars and fifteen years trying to hold onto whatever part of the *Atocha* he could? It took him longer to fight the state than to find the wreck."

I didn't know where his melancholy was coming from, but thought Susan McLeash might be perfect to pick up his spirits. "You want to go after the state, I have a way."

"You got that damned right. I won't be getting any of my cut after that damned lawyer was found in Gross's garage. Between Gross's greedy daughter and the state, there'll be nothing left. I'm all about revenge."

"You said DeWitt hung around some bars that you know? I have a nice woman who works with me that would love to take you out drinking."

The cigar straightened in his mouth. "Now that's a worthwhile assignment."

Now I just had to find Susan and convince her that hanging around with someone who resembled a vagrant would help her career. "Maybe we ought to head back to your place and see what we can do to clean you up."

"Another one of those pills'll fix me."

I ignored the request and started back to the truck. He took two steps and started feigning pain that was so bad he couldn't walk. "I'll get the truck," I said, walking away without waiting for a response.

Once I was out of earshot, I pulled my phone out, found Susan's contact info, and pressed connect. I worked on my story while it rang and was about to give up when she picked up.

"Martinez told me we would be working together," she said.

"Got plans for the evening?" I asked. From the background noise, I could tell she wasn't home.

"Always open to a better offer," she said.

I explained the importance of finding DeWitt and that I had a CI who knew where he hung out.

"A CI, huh?"

I sensed she was going to turn me down. It was time to sweeten the pot. "He's supposed to be hanging around with these treasure hunters and their backers."

I wasn't sure which of the two groups I mentioned were more important, but suspected it was the backers that got her attention.

"When and where?"

Chapter 17

On the way back to Slipstream's apartment I grilled him about where DeWitt hung out. He had already told me the bar at the Miami Beach Marina was one spot, but I was hoping for somewhere I wasn't known. We arrived at his building and went upstairs. He'd given me the names of several other places that I checked out on my phone while he changed clothes. I had Susan on standby, so if Martinez didn't do his part, which I suspected from the late hour that he wouldn't, I would have to make the call.

I had to admit I was surprised when Slipstream came out of his bedroom. "Not bad," I said, looking him over. The floral print Hawaiian shirt was at least clean and his shorts were a decent match. He had shaved and his hair was combed back. With a fresh cigar dangling from his mouth he looked less like a worn-out deckhand and actually pretty respectable. A cane to go along with his walking boot would have completed the outfit nicely, but I was pretty happy with what we had. I tossed him a pill for his efforts, which he happily gobbled down. Susan was enough to put a sloth on edge; hopefully the pill would keep him in check.

It was getting close to six and with still no word from Martinez, I decided to write him off for the night. It was surprising enough to have found him still working until five. Past that hour was out of the question. I chose the nicest looking place from the list that Slipstream had given me and texted Susan the name and address. She responded with a smiley face emoji.

"Okay," I said, handing him two twenties. "This is it. You better make it last."

"I ain't getting you no receipt from a bar."

I nodded, figuring that as long as Susan was

involved Martinez would reimburse me either way. "And watch your language. Let her do the talking."

"So, is she hot or what? You didn't fix me up with a dog, did you?"

"I think you'll get along just fine." It was time to head out. With the bathroom finally vacant, I used it to change my shirt to a button-down that I had in the truck. The Park Service pants were plain khaki and without the uniform shirt, I would blend in. There was no way I was leaving these two together without a chaperone, especially when alcohol was involved. We left the apartment and headed down to the truck. On the way downstairs, I noticed the parking lot had emptied out from its near-capacity state earlier.

"Damn, we're going upscale," he said when he saw where we were going.

"Only the best for you, my friend." I had chosen the place to get Susan interested. And if Maria was really involved with DeWitt, she wasn't the type to slum it. It was a big place on the mainland side of the

Intracoastal Waterway up toward Miami Beach; a little more old school and blue blood than the trendier South Beach. Surrounded by several marinas, the restaurant had a sign that boasted of both an indoor and an outdoor bar, as well as outside seating.

Parking was scarce, forcing me to leave the truck with a valet. It cost me an extra twenty to have him park it somewhere I could gain access to it myself and keep the key. I was burning through non-reimbursable twenties at an alarming rate, but with my gun belt in the glove compartment and the possibility of needing the truck for a quick exit, it justified the cost.

We stayed to the side of several groups of people waiting for a table. Slipstream kept peering inside, but I wanted them to enter together. A few minutes later I saw Susan walking toward us. She wore a sundress that was a little too tight in what I thought were all the wrong places, and the usual application of makeup that was heavy enough to weigh down her head. From the crooked smile and squint in her eyes, I could tell she had not been home when I called. Watching her approach, I judged that she was in the perfect state of mind for Slipstream.

"And who's this?" she asked.

The words were not slurred; a good sign. "Slipstream, this is Susan." I introduced the couple. She reached out for his hand, which I took as another good sign. "Why don't you two go in and check the place out? I'll hang back." Because both Maria and DeWitt knew me, I would have to be careful if they were here.

I watched Slipstream and Susan enter the restaurant, surprised when he opened the door for her. They giggled about something and I relaxed slightly; at least for now things were under control, but I knew with the two of them and alcohol in the mix—never mind the pill I had given Slipstream— this could go sideways at any time. For now, they appeared to be on equal footing.

Moving to the side of the crowd, I pulled out my phone and checked to see if Martinez had called. There were no missed calls, text messages, or emails. I was surprised there were no texts from Allie, who usually sent an emoji every time her mood changed. The stupid characters had advanced my age, making me carry reading glasses to be able to see the different faces and know if she was happy or sad. Checking again, I was about to call her when I remembered I had given her the number for my new personal phone.

I had left it in the truck, half-expecting that Martinez might have some kind of technology sniffer incorporated into his surveillance. Glancing back at the entrance to the restaurant several times along the way, I walked back to the truck and retrieved the phone. The notification screen was full of smiley faces and I typed a quick message that I loved her, but was working and would call her later. Seconds after I sent the message the phone dinged with another smiley face.

With the screen littered with emojis, I almost didn't see the missed call on the bottom. I recognized the number immediately. Hoping I hadn't blown my window of opportunity, I hit the number.

"Thought I lost you there, Hunter."

"Mac, thanks for calling back. Got another phone, it's complicated."

"You're telling me. Any luck with your investigation?"

I gave him the thirty-second update.

"Those GPS numbers might be worth watching. If that anchor was cut, someone has them. They're not going to wait for this to blow over. One storm can cover up a season's work. Some things need to be done fast and hard."

That kind of went back to Slipstream's rant about the state and archeologists being involved. It seemed the licensing process was so long that some of the wrecks could be destroyed or disappear before a permit was issued. I totally got preserving history, but retrieving them from the clutches of the ocean did not allow for the same timeline as reclaiming an ancient city from the jungle or fossils from the ground.

"Any interest in coming up here?" If there was one person I could trust with the numbers, it was Mac.

"Been thinking about it. Maybe I can grab Tru and make the run tomorrow."

The thought of Trufante and Slipstream together sent a shiver up my spine. Watching one was damned near a full-time job. "We can use my Park Service boat if you want to drive up," I told him.

He paused for a minute. "Might be the best way to check them out. My boat'll stand out up there."

We made plans to meet at the headquarters building at seven in the morning, giving me a solid hour's safety margin before Martinez showed up. My work phone vibrated, and I juggled the two phones for a second, thanking him and checking the message on the other phone at the same time. The text was from Susan: a picture of DeWitt sitting next to Maria.

A second later it dinged again. "This guy's getting creepy." I guessed the honeymoon was over. Now that we had located DeWitt and Maria I wondered what to do. I was sure Miami-Dade would want both for questioning and I couldn't ignore the BOLO. Hoping it would gain me a few points, I called Grace and gave her our location.

I texted Susan that help was on the way and to have another drink and hang in there. If they had seen Slipstream, they hadn't bolted. The last thing I needed was for DeWitt to get suspicious, but in case he did I moved closer to the entrance.

Fifteen minutes later, an unmarked police car pulled up in front. It skidded to a stop, and before it even stopped rolling Traynor had popped out of the driver's seat and flashed his badge at the valet attendant. Clearly not wanting a confrontation, the valet raised his hands and backed away. A second later, Grace opened the passenger door, called something to Traynor, and came toward me.

"What's the situation?"

I would have preferred more of a "how do you want to handle it" attitude, but this was their territory. I showed her the picture of the happy couple, and told her that Slipstream and Susan were inside.

"Do we have enough on this guy to make an arrest?"

"I got nothing, besides seeing him lurking around Gross's garage."

She looked at the picture again. "They look pretty comfortable to me."

I was just about to speak when Traynor pushed between us.

"We gonna make an arrest, or what?"

I looked over at Grace, hoping she was going to break the bad news to him. Before either of us could offer an explanation there was a disturbance just inside the doorway. Slipstream was the first outside, followed by DeWitt. They looked like they were about to start throwing punches.

Pushing past Grace and Traynor, I went to separate the two men, but Susan stumbled through the door with her gun extended. A movement behind me caught my attention and glancing back I saw that Traynor had his gun drawn as well. Several of the patrons waiting for tables started to scream and pushed their way past us in an attempt to escape.

"She's my partner," I shouted at Traynor. "Both of you put down your weapons." I glared back and forth at each of them until finally, they backed off. Traynor's pistol went back into his shoulder holster. Susan's small revolver went someplace I would rather not describe.

"The guy went after me," Slipstream said.

He was slurring now and I wondered if he had burned through the entire forty dollars in the ten minutes they had been inside. I looked back to where DeWitt had been standing. He was gone. Again.

The restaurant was elevated enough for me to see out over the parking lot. There was no sign of him there. Looking to either side, I saw the slips adjacent to the restaurant and caught sight of a man and woman running fast toward one of the docks. I took off after them, pushing past the panicked customers.

DeWitt had the tall, lean body of a runner and he quickly outpaced me. Maria was surprisingly fast. I had been an athlete of sorts in my youth, and had been working hard on the paddleboard with Justine, but between living on an island and spending most of my time in boats. Between the lead they had and my paddler's legs were no match for his.

They disappeared behind a building and before I could reach it, I heard the almost simultaneous sound of twin outboards starting. By the time I reached the dock, all I could see was the transom of a large center console speeding down the Intracoastal

Chapter 18

"How the hell could you let them get away?" Traynor was in Susan's face. "Headline: Park Service agents lose treasure hunter's killer."

As much as I would have liked to see them go at it, I stepped between them, scowled at Traynor, and grabbed Susan's arm. She fought me, but I could tell it was for show.

"It was that nimrod's fault. Where did you find that guy? He touched me inappropriately."

"And you made a scene. DeWitt saw it and bolted."

She nodded, but the look on her face was nowhere near an apology. "Where is that weasel?"

The entrance to the restaurant was still clear. The groups that had been waiting for tables were huddled out of harm's way, gesturing and speculating as to what had happened. Traynor was in Grace's face; she was on her phone.

I walked Susan to a bench and asked her to wait, then approached the detectives. "Maybe we ought to clear out of here before someone tips off the press that this was related to Gross's murder?"

Grace nodded and, still on the phone, walked down the short flight of stairs to the sidewalk. With a scowl, she looked back at her partner, who followed. I stepped in next to him. "Susan McLeash is a special agent working with me. I expect you to treat her properly."

"It was the heat of the moment." He looked at her, sitting on the bench. "I'll go play nice." He moved toward her. I could only see his back, but there must have been something that allowed Susan to let down her guard. Seconds later they were sitting next to each other and chatting like old friends. Maybe she had another purpose after all, I thought, as I turned my attention away from them and walked over to Grace.

"Got two boats in pursuit," she said.

That was the right call. There was nothing for us to do besides wait here to keep a lookout and ensure that they didn't backtrack and head out to Government Cut or into the bay. One pursuing boat would likely take the river and the other the Intracoastal. I thought about calling my friend Johnny Wells with ICE, but unless I knew they were going international on us, there was not a lot he could do. As long as the search stayed in the Intracoastal, Miami-Dade had jurisdiction. Knowing a few of their captains, I judged they weren't likely to accept help.

"Looks like you lost your CI," Grace said.

I looked around the parking lot and entrance. Things had returned to normal and she was right—there was no sign of him. I did have an idea, though, and told her I would be right back. Entering the restaurant, I walked past the hostess stand to the bar and immediately saw him sitting there drinking on my money. I walked over and put my hand on his shoulder.

"That didn't go so well, huh?" he asked, quickly finishing his drink.

"I gather that Susan was not impressed?" I didn't wait for an answer. Grabbing his arm, I escorted him outside. There were two police cruisers parked out front now. The officers were milling around and talking to Grace. With no desire to navigate the personal and political quagmire going on in front of the restaurant, I found Susan and asked her to stay here and watch for the boat while I took Slipstream home. She seemed happy to be sitting with Traynor and agreed.

"Come on." I led Slipstream to the truck.

"Where we going?"

"Home. I think you've had enough for the night." The combination of the pill and the forty dollars of alcohol was evident. I figured one more pill would put him down for the night, out of my, and harm's, way.

"What about DeWitt?"

"The police have two boats looking for him."

"He's a slippery bastard," he said, hauling his walking boot into the truck. He sat back and exhaled after the effort, then took the chewed-up cigar out of his mouth and peeled off the end. "Him and Gross's daughter are up to something."

I had to agree with that, but I had no desire to talk about the case with him. Things were percolating in my head. Pieces of the puzzle looked like they should fit together, but didn't. There was an answer there and I just had to find it. Unfortunately it was too late to fish.

As I drove, I thought about the metaphorical jigsaw puzzle. Motive appeared easy here: treasure. I supposed if I could actually locate the people involved I could check out their alibis, but one was dead and two were missing. The only ones left available were Slipstream and Gail Gross. I had to admit I was stuck.

The apartment complex was a flurry of activity. Music blasted from boom boxes and people were gathered around the balcony that ran around Slipstream's building. Glancing at my watch I saw it was almost nine, and it looked like the party was just getting going. After I pulled up in front of the stairs to his unit, Slipstream gave me a sorry look and I fished the pill bottle out of my pocket. I handed him one and watched as he limped upstairs. As he disappeared into his unit, I wondered if he was becoming more of a liability than an asset.

Pulling back onto 836, I decided to call it a night and headed south toward headquarters. I texted Justine and got a sad face emoji in reply. It was hard being newlyweds and having two homes, but I had to meet Mac Travis in the morning and in my present mood, I was probably better off alone. I thought about getting up early and fishing for a few hours before meeting Mac. Maybe that would put things in perspective.

Just before I pulled onto the Turnpike, my phone rang. It sat on the seat next to me and I was able to see the caller ID. I had seen the number before but couldn't place it. With nothing to lose, I picked up the phone.

"Agent Hunter, this is Jim DeWitt with the state."

He said it like he had done nothing wrong. I let him continue.

"We need to talk."

"You know you ran from the police, not once, but twice, and there is a BOLO out for you and Maria."

"You don't understand. I'm running my own investigation here. We're stepping on each other's toes."

I wasn't quite sure how an underwater

archeologist was running an investigation, but I was game to find out. "This has to be between us. If the detectives working with me find out about this, there'll be hell to pay."

"The last thing I want to do is talk to the locals."

Of course it was. Investigation or not, they would put him in jail first and sort out the details later. "I'm by 836 and the Turnpike. Where do you want to meet?" I was hoping for a public place. He gave me the name of a restaurant and we agreed on thirty minutes.

I pulled off at the next exit and entered the restaurant's name into the maps app. It showed it was ten minutes away, leaving me an extra twenty minutes before I had to meet him. Following the directions, I reversed course, but turned onto 836 toward Miami instead of following the Turnpike. I wasn't going to involve Grace, but I wasn't going alone either.

Ten minutes later, I pulled up at the forensics

lab and texted Justine. After she agreed to take a break and go with me, I had a moment's doubt about involving her. We had worked several cases before and I had no worries about her in the field. It was her working for Miami-Dade that had me concerned now, and I hoped this was not going to be a conflict of interest for her.

When she got in the car, she must have seen the troubled expression on my face. "What's up?"

I told her what had happened at the restaurant and got the look I'd expected when I mentioned Susan McLeash's name. Justine was not a fan— originally, she had doubted me, thinking that I was paranoid about Susan's behavior, but it hadn't taken long for her to see the truth.

"You need to upgrade your team."

She was right about that.

"DeWitt wants to meet. I have reservations about going alone and I can't bring in Grace. Are you going to get in trouble if you go with me?"

She thought about it for less time than it took me to ask. "Heck yeah, I'm in."

"You sure?"

"I'm officially on break. Let's go stealth and take my car and leave your work phone and truck here."

It was interesting how even someone as dedicated as she was could partition her life. I wished I could do the same. "Now you're talking." The freedom from Martinez's surveillance was still new enough to be novel. I locked the truck and took a last look at the phone left behind on the passenger seat.

Justine drove to the restaurant and we parked. Checking my new personal phone, I saw we were five minutes early. I didn't want to blindside DeWitt with Justine, so we agreed that I would wait by the entrance for him and then call for her.

A moment later, a white SUV pulled in. The parking lot lights were bright enough that I could see him scanning the lot for my truck. He parked and I waited while he locked the SUV and came toward me.

"Oh, there you are. Didn't see your truck," he said.

"I don't know about the state, but the feds have trackers in everything."

He looked at me like he didn't have any idea what I was talking about. "Fine. I'm all for being careful."

I could only hope that Miami-Dade wasn't tracking his SUV right now and were on their way, ready to interrupt our meeting. I thought about asking him to move his vehicle, but with Justine on break our time was limited and I didn't want to freak him out.

"I've got Justine from the crime lab with me. She's my wife, actually. You okay with that?"

"Yeah," he said.

According to his job description DeWitt was a scientist as well. They would likely find some common ground. That worked for me and I waved to Justine. She met us at the entrance.

Seated at a booth in the back corner, I waited to speak until the waitress brought our drinks. DeWitt eyed the menu as if he wanted to order something, but this meeting wasn't going to last that long especially if his eating ritual was anywhere near as complicated as his coffee one.

"You wanted to talk?"

"Right. Look, I've got no hard feelings, but I am running an autonomous investigation for the state." He said this as if he was with the FBI, then pulled a piece of paper out of his pocket and handed it to me like a peace offering.

"What's this?"

"A list of Gross's competitors. You know, the guys that might benefit from his death."

It was a transparent attempt to deflect the investigation away from himself. I took the paper, glanced at the names, refolded it, and put it in my pocket.

"If you want to find them all in one place, Vince Bugarra has an extravaganza planned for tomorrow afternoon on the beach at the Savoy."

"And they're all going to be there?"

"His parties are not to be missed. You want to see fundraising, bring the family and check it out."

Chapter 19

We left the restaurant and went our separate ways. I wondered if, by telling me about the party and giving me the list of names, he was trying to muddy the waters. What I needed to do was to figure out why.

I still planned to head to Adams Key and explained my reasons to Justine on the way back to the lab. She was in the middle of her shift and would be working until midnight. Mac and I planned to meet at seven. I knew she wanted to come along, but it would be a logistical nightmare. Instead we made plans to attend the party together.

My phone rang about ten minutes after I'd dropped her off.

"If you're still around, you should come down here," Justine said.

"I'm close. Be there in ten." I made a U turn at the next intersection and headed back toward the crime lab, wondering what she was so excited about.

She met me at the security door just inside the entrance to the lab. It had taken some time for both of us to get comfortable with the new facility. Working the swing shift, Justine had staked out the old lab as her domain after the day shift had moved into the new one. We had enjoyed some of our formative moments in that lab and I think we both missed it.

Things were different in the new lab. For one thing, we seldom had privacy, and as we walked past the smoked glass floor-to-ceiling windows I could see lights still on at several workstations. Justine had been resistant—or maybe stubborn—but when she'd gotten a look at the new equipment lined up on gleaming stainless steel tables, she knew her forensics firepower had been upgraded from peashooter to bazooka. That had made the move to the new lab easier to accept.

The glass door opened automatically when she swiped her card. We entered the lab and I followed her to her workstation. "They finally let me process the garage at Gross's house. After the crowd thinned out, I got into his office, too."

There were two distinct piles on the table, one, I guessed, from each area. "Anything you can share about Morehead's murder?" It was Miami-Dade's case—I had to ask.

"Pretty straightforward. Blunt force trauma to the head."

"I don't remember any sign of a struggle. Any weapon?"

"Nothing was out of place. He must have known and trusted the murderer to turn his back on him."

The garage had been where Gross processed his finds. It looked like a meeting had taken place where Gross had been showing his backer what he had found. She must have read my mind.

"Looks like Gross, at least until I can run the prints. Hopefully there's something conclusive there, because the DNA is going to get the back burner with the prime suspect also dead."

"What about a time of death? It would have to be before Gross was killed."

"Sid thought it was at least a day earlier."

When things fell that neatly into place, I tended to worry. She hadn't called me down here to show me this; therc had to be more.

"So," shc paused, letting the tension build. "The more interesting items were in his office." She pulled one of the piles toward us. A folded chart caught my eye, but she pushed that away and placed several bank statements sealed in plastic bags in front of me.

"Unless he has a pile of Spanish gold buried somewhere, he was in trouble." It only took a few minutes to see the declining balances in his accounts over the last several months. There were three bank accounts that showed a combined net worth of less than a thousand dollars. "Looks like he barely had gas money. I don't remember any artifacts around the house either."

"For the setup he had in the garage, there was surprisingly little material in process."

I had my doubts about Gross being the killer. It made sense that he had used the lure of gold to get Morehead to come over, then killed him. His financial situation could have turned on a dime if he didn't need to split the money with his backer. But, the body still lying there a day later pointed to someone else who was trying to implicate Gross. "So, we have a broke treasure hunter who apparently wasn't killed for his treasure, and a dead backer who hadn't gotten a return on his investment." I wondered again about the state paperwork and if it jived with what we had found. I didn't expect those records would be forthcoming; aside from giving me Bugarra's party list, DeWitt was hardly cooperating.

Dealing with the state bureaucracy was not in my wheelhouse and Martinez was apparently all talk. In the morning, I would ask Mariposa if she could charm her way through the state's defenses.

Justine had moved to a piece of equipment that I couldn't even begin to guess what its purpose was, and looked anxious to get back to work. I snuck a goodnight kiss and left the building.

The ride back to headquarters was a blur; nothing made sense. There had to be something else. I could only hope that tomorrow, between the rendezvous with Mac and the fundraiser, would prove more productive.

Even the ride across the bay couldn't set my mind straight. Usually, no matter where my head was, the feeling of the boat getting up on plane and gliding across the water put a smile on my face, but not tonight. There was a fair breeze blowing directly in my face, and I had to work the throttle to avoid slamming the bow into the oncoming waves. Wet and tired, I reached Adams Key, where Gross's boat was still tied off to the dock.

The concrete dock had been built to accommodate Ray's and my Park Service boats, as well as a handful of craft that used it to access the day-use area to the west of our houses. I tied off in front of the converted sportfisher and headed up to my house. Thankfully, Zero missed my entrance—or maybe he sensed that I was alone.

Stocking a kitchen on an island is problematic, usually requiring a trip that meant transiting the bay and driving another eight miles to the closest grocery store. There was little in the pantry and only fish, eggs, and beer in the refrigerator. Neither of the foodstuffs sounded good, so I grabbed a beer and headed to the bathroom to shower off the spray from the ride over.

Just as I had undressed, I heard a knock on the door—a very unusual occurrence out here. Hoping it wasn't a boater looking for help, I pulled my shorts back on and went to answer it.

Zero barged in ahead of Ray. With his nails slipping and scraping on the tile floor, he did a thorough search of the house for Justine and Allie. When he turned up neither, he collapsed onto the floor by the couch, panting heavily. I left him to his loneliness and turned to Ray.

"What's up?" I asked, wondering why he was here, though I had my suspicions. It was after nine; not late by many standards, but he was a crack-of-dawn kind of guy. This was past his bedtime. Several loud snores from Zero indicated that he felt the same way.

"Any luck with the Gross case?" he asked.

"Hold on." I usually set the thermostat in the eighties, but after being outside in the humid air the air-conditioning was sending a chill through me. I went back to the bedroom and grabbed my shirt and my beer. Without having to ask if he wanted one, I went to the refrigerator and took out another, opened it, and handed it to Ray.

"Found one of his backers dead this morning." Everything I was about to tell him had probably been on the evening news. There was no harm, and I thought stating the facts out loud might sort things out for me. I went through the events that had taken place since the other night, when I had seen him aboard the *Reale*. The only thing I left out was the revelation about Gross's finances.

"Those state bureaucrats are as bad as the feds."

I agreed and we drank and commiserated for a few minutes, knowing first-hand how bad it could get after working for Martinez. As we talked, I loosened up a little. Having Ray as an ally was important. Aside from being my only neighbor, he was a good guy and trustworthy, though I had to include "generally" to that assessment after seeing him skulking around the boat the other night.

"What do you have going on tomorrow?" I asked. Unlike myself, as long as the out islands were running right and there were no complaints from the rangers that ran the campgrounds on Boca Chita and Elliot Keys, Ray was free to do what he wanted. I thought it would be a no-brainer that he would want to go with Mac and I.

"Got a small list, but nothing urgent."

"Mac Travis, a salvage guy from down in the Keys, is coming up in the morning. We were planning on trying to recreate Gross's last day—interested?"

His eyes lit up. Even his love for fishing was diminished by any mention of treasure. "You bet. I remember you talking about that guy."

"Solid as they come. Doesn't say much, though."

"That'll make for a quiet day with the three of us. How're you planning on figuring out where he was at?"

"Okay, before we go any further, I have to tell you when I saw you aboard Gross's boat the other night I thought you were checking out his GPS." It felt good to get it out in the open.

He shrugged. It was an off-hand admission of guilt. He knew that I knew, and that was good enough.

"I could show you a few tricks with the GPS, but someone took it off the boat."

I went back to my bedroom to retrieve it. "I couldn't find anything on it near the location I found the boat."

"You good if we go down and hook it back up? There's an interface with the depth finder that might tell us something."

Marine electronics were still new to me. I knew enough to know that my Park Service bay boat was minimally equipped. The chart plotter with its built-in depth finder was all I needed to navigate the bay. The VHF radio became easy once I learned the correct stations for different types of communication. Though what I had was satisfactory, I remembered getting boat envy when I'd seen the cluttered dashboard of Johnny Wells's forty-foot Interceptor with its radar and other equipment.

I grabbed two fresh beers and with the GPS under my arm, we went downstairs. Zero cracked an eyelid when he heard the door, but decided to stay in the air-conditioned house. At the dock, we boarded Gross's boat, reattached the unit to its mount, and reconnected the transducer and power cable. Unlike the chart plotter on my boat, Gross had separate instruments for each function.

While the unit started up, Ray went to the depth finder and turned the power on. It had a much larger screen than any that I had seen before and as he scrolled through the settings, I saw several different views. He continued to work through the unit until he found what he wanted.

"This shows the bottom track from his last day, starting at six a.m."

"How's that going to help?"

He explained to me how the scrolling display

was time-stamped. As we moved quickly through the readings, the bottom appeared generally flat for several minutes before I saw a series of single spikes and a bulge.

"Doesn't look like a wreck." I stared at the lines.

"Anything out of the normal is something." Ray stopped the display and pressed his finger on the screen at the mid-point of the anomaly. "There you go," he said, pointing to the top right corner of the display, where the coordinates of the spot were displayed.

Chapter 20

Ray was in full Martinez-avoidance mode when I met him at the dock the next morning. It was probably better that I went alone to pick up Mac anyway. He had texted a half hour before, when he'd left Marathon and, wanting to avoid the cameras at headquarters, we agreed to meet at the fuel dock across the way. I timed my trip to meet him and left the dock at Adams Key about an hour later.

It looked as if it would be another stellar day on the bay. Once the season turned at the end of September, it knocked a few degrees off the day-time highs and the mornings were noticeably cooler. Unless something was brewing in the tropics, the wind was generally less than during the more turbulent spring.

With the sun at my back, I cruised over the small ripples on the surface, which the deep V on the hull easily parted, rearranged, and spread into the long wake streaming behind the boat. It was too early to see the shades of the water, or rather the bottom through the clear water, but I had a smile on my face and was over my melancholy from last night.

Cases tended to hit dry patches, and the last few days had been Sahara dry. I didn't have much, but at least finding the trail from Gross's depth finder gave us a new direction.

Justine and I had talked before I went to bed last night. I'd told her about the anomaly on the depth finder and my plan to check it out with Mac this morning. I knew she wanted to go, too, but changed the subject to the fundraiser this afternoon. She was frustrated by the evidence collected from Gross's garage and office and thought the event might be a good opportunity to snag some DNA or fingerprints. It would have to be cleared through her supervisor, but collecting prints and samples was case-related and she didn't expect any problems.

I pulled up to the gas dock at Bayfront Park a few minutes before seven. Not sure how far we were going to run today, I figured it wouldn't hurt to top off the tank. Mac and I had also decided it was better to meet here. The ten-dollar parking fee was well worth being able to stay clear of Martinez's surveillance cameras.

Looking down the seawall, I watched the flow of traffic going in and out of the ramp. There were about half as many boats coming in after catching bait or spending the night fishing the reef as those heading out. The boats and trailers moved in and out of the water like clockwork. This wouldn't be the case in a few hours, when the amateurs descended on the park.

I heard the sound of a supercharged diesel before I saw the light blue vehicle pull up. The heavyweight predecessor to what we call an SUV looked to be rebuilt. The newer clear-coat embellished the old rust-streaked surface and when he pulled around I saw the barn-style back door in place of a tailgate.

A minute after finding a parking space, Mac climbed down from the lifted chassis set up on 35-inch mud tires. The boat was still taking fuel, so I waved my free hand in his direction. He went to the back of the truck and pulled out a large duffle and came toward me.

"Hey, nice ride."

"Belongs to a buddy of mine, Jesse McDermitt. He calls it the Beast."

That about fit. The overflow from the gas tank started to gurgle and I carefully released the handle, tapping the nozzle on the lip of the inlet and handing it up to the waiting attendant. While he totaled up the charge, I took Mac's bag and set it in the bow, just forward of the cooler in front of the console.

He climbed down and we shook hands without

the fashionable man-hug. After seeing Martinez trying to pull that off at a press conference, I thought a handshake alone would suffice. The attendant handed me a clipboard. After signing the receipt, I handed it back and started the engine. Mac dropped the lines, tossed them back onto the dock, and pushed us off the seawall.

I have never been to war, but I've been in some bad situations. One of those had been with Mac down in the Keys. Going through a life-or-death experience with someone creates a unique bond. We hadn't said two complete sentences, but I felt totally at ease with him as we coasted over the waves on the way back to Adams Key.

Ray was waiting for us and helped with the lines. Mac and I climbed onto the dock and I introduced him to Zero first, who pushed his fifty-pound bowling ball-shaped body between us, and then to Ray.

"What d'ya got?" Mac asked.

He said that the same way that John Wayne had once said *We're burning daylight*. He walked down the dock to Gross's boat and hopped aboard without waiting for an answer. A minute later, a cloud of black smoke drifted above the stern when the engines started.

He stayed at the helm for a few minutes then leaned outboard from the open window. "Any reason we can't take this?"

I hadn't thought about using Gross's boat. It was a crime scene, but Justine had already processed it. Sitting here at the dock, it was subject to the same weather conditions as it would be out on the water, and it was certainly the better craft for what we had planned. Finally, I decided there was no harm, though Martinez might have a problem when he got in the office and checked the camera mounted on the pole above the security light. I was in all-out passive-aggressive mode anyway after he hadn't helped track DeWitt, so I pulled my bag out of the console and carried it over to the larger boat.

We loaded our gear. While Ray checked and secured the tanks, I showed Mac what we had found on the depth finder last night. He played with the GPS for a minute and confirmed there was no track recorded from Gross's last trip. The couple of waypoints from Morehead's computer and the anomaly on the depth finder were all we had. I wondered if there was a match, but that would be too easy. I pulled my phone out and opened the picture I had taken of Morehead's spreadsheet. They were three separate spots.

Once we were underway, I was glad we had taken the larger boat. Three men on the twenty-two footer, with all our tanks and diving gear, would have been a tight fit. I let Ray run the boat while Mac and I moved two folding deck chairs out back and caught up on our lives. Once we were clear of the shallow bank to the north of Caesar Creek, Ray accelerated and it turned into mostly nodding and not a lot of talking; not that I would expect more than that from the two of us anyway.

At twenty knots, the boat seemed to find her sea legs. The engine noise went down and the ride leveled out. Elliot Key, then Sands and Boca Chita passed by on the port side. We were soon in open water, and Ray turned seaward of Stiltsville, setting a course for the coordinates. Avoiding the ramshackle water-bound neighborhood was always a good thing. The fate of Stiltsville was one of the few things that Martinez and I agreed on, both hoping a storm or legislative act would eventually erase it from the water. For him it was a maintenance nightmare; for me the seven remaining buildings were only trouble.

After listening to the engines run for another few minutes, I could feel the rpms drop and the hull settle in the water. Mac and I rose and went to the helm. It was crowded with three heads around the electronics and I backed away, letting the two more experienced men handle things.

"I'll go forward and take care of the anchor," I said, stepping up to the raised deck that covered the interior cabin. Using the rail to guide myself, I reached the bow and unclipped the safety lanyard with the replacement rode and anchor that Ray had installed. Unlike my boat, where manpower was required to set and retrieve the anchor, the *Reale* had a windlass that did the work for you.

I could feel the boat turn into the wind and then start to circle, slowly closing the diameter with each turn. Finally, the engines reversed and Ray called out to drop anchor. I stepped back and watched as the chain slid through the guide. He seemed to sense when the free fall stopped and the anchor hit bottom, then backed down, further allowing the movement of the boat to pull out another hundred feet of line. When he stopped the boat started to swing and with the waves now coming directly toward the bow, I knew we were hooked and tied off the line.

Ray cut the engines and we stood around the electronics, staring at the clutter on the screen. It looked identical to what we had seen last night.

"Let's go see what we've got," Mac said, making a move for the deck.

Within minutes we were geared up. One at a time we took a giant stride off the dive platform and entered the water. Mac and Ray were much more experienced than I. They quickly spun and with their heads to the depths started toward the anchor line. I followed, clearing my ears every few feet. The current was strong and I soon saw both men adjust their trajectory a few degrees and head directly to the bottom. Once we cleared thirty feet, the current lessened and I could see several dark shapes starting to form below me.

My first instinct was to swim directly for whatever was down there, but with no one on the boat, it was prudent to check the anchor. Passing by the dark spot, we were soon grouped around the anchor and each gave the okay signal.

The surface current had worked in our favor and the anchor was deeply embedded in the sandy bottom. Mac was the first to move away, with Ray and I following. With the amount of scope Ray had let out, we had to cross about a hundred feet of desert, but halfway there I could see something start to rise above the sea floor.

I'd dove on several wrecks before and knew better than to have set expectations, especially when the origin was unknown. Even then, it was a surprise to see a smokestack projecting from the bottom with clusters of fish around it. I saw Ray turn and eye the large school of yellowtail, and I knew he was filing the location away in his mind for a future trip.

From its dimensions, it looked like what we had seen on the depth finder. A vague outline of a ship lay below us—not an intact wreck, but iron and steel fittings left over from a wooden ship, and one more modern than I had expected. We approached from the stern. Following Mac, we started around the wreck. I estimated it at a little over a hundred and fifty feet long. The wooden supports and sheathing had long decayed or been eaten by worms, leaving a trail of metal components. The railing that had once circumnavigated the ship lay in sections, giving the wreck its shape.

With Gross's name attached, I had expected a long-lost Spanish galleon. If that had been the case we would have been looking at little more than a pile of ballast stones and maybe some artillery. In these waters the wood-seeking Teredo worm needed only a fraction of the four or five centuries since the ship had sunk to consume the hull.

Several iron or steel masts lay askew on the seafloor. I swam over to one and studied it, then moved toward the interior of the wreck. What was left was well-entrenched in the sand and it would take some research to figure out which vessel it had been, but it was clear what it wasn't. In hindsight, I wished we had brought a camera to help document it and determine its origin.

After circling the wreck, we moved over the interior sections. Because it lay flat on the sandy bottom it was no wonder the depth finder had only shown the stack.

My dive computer beeped when we fell to seventy feet, past the dive profile that I had created. It also showed we had been down for thirty minutes. With only a thousand PSI left in my tank, I ascended to fifty feet, hoping the shallower depth would help with my air consumption and extend the dive.

Mac moved toward a large piece of metal that projected a few feet from the bottom. Circling overhead, I guessed from its shape that it had been the boiler. Ray finned to a large square feature that was elevated above the seafloor. It had probably been the frame for a long gone wooden hatch. He started searching around that area.

Another look at my air gauge showed I was

down to 500 PSI. I assumed, being more experienced, that Ray and Mac would have more air, and not wanting to be *that guy* and cut the dive short, I shot some air in my BC and rose another ten feet above the bottom. I slowly circled the wreck, trying to use as little energy as possible while committing the features to memory.

The upper half of Ray's body had disappeared into the frame, leaving only his legs and a bubble trail to show where he was. Mac continued to move around the wreck, stopping every so often to examine something. Despite my attempts to conserve air, the needle was pegged deep in the red and I released a brass clip from my BC. Just as I reached behind me to smack the aluminum tank and get their attention, I saw Ray pull his body back and start toward the surface. He clearly held something in his hand.

Chapter 21

"Looks like a munition," Mac said.

We were gathered around the cylindrical object that Ray had brought up. The air compressor purred quietly in the background, refilling the tanks; another perk of using Gross's boat. After removing our gear, I had used my phone to do an image search for the kind of ship it might be. "Looks like around the Civil War." I passed the phone to Mac, who nodded and handed it to Ray.

"I'd agree. Iron or steel stack and boiler, same for the masts, would indicate its vintage."

"It's certainly not a Spanish galleon," Ray said. The disappointment was evident in his voice.

Mac took a deep breath. "These kind of ships transported a lot of goods and money. Treasure hunting is not always about Spanish gold. Think about it. If you're out to make money at this game, salvage of any kind that nets a profit is what you need to focus on. Instead of searching for the decayed bones of four-hundred-year-old wooden ships that barely register on a magnetometer, why not focus on something that's easier to find and can pay the bills?"

I had been a little disappointed as well, but Mac was right and I needed to remember that I was here to find a murderer, not discover treasure. My watch showed we had been on the surface for thirty minutes. We had decided on a ninety-minute break before diving again, to allow the nitrogen to dissipate from our bloodstreams and to also allow us about the same bottom time as the first dive. Scrolling through the settings, the computer showed almost an hour of no-decompression bottom time for our second dive if we waited that long.

Something in the corner of my eye distracted me and I scanned the water, checking for boats and storms—something I should have been doing automatically. My eyes found a school of birds crashing the surface not far away. The water was churned up and small silver humps reflected the sunlight when the fishes' backs broke the surface as they chased the baitfish. I looked over at Ray and Mac, who had seen them as well. Otherwise it looked like the horizon was clear of any storms, nor were there any signs of the huge, anvil-shaped clouds forming that would bring them.

October is what the locals call a "shoulder season" here. Midway between the beginning of school and the start of the winter season, the area became almost devoid of tourists. When the weather was as nice as today's, the locals took advantage, and there were several boats out. A few were heading to the deeper reef or offshore to fish, but there seemed to be a steady stream going in the direction of the Fowey Rocks Lighthouse, which looked about half its true height on the horizon.

The first in the chain of steel beacons that marked the reef and extended to Key West was a prime snorkeling and diving spot. Some boats, probably seeing the huge blowers now in their upright position on the stern of the *Reale*, moved in for a closer look—closer than I would have liked. This boat was like bait. With its winches and blowers, it looked like what it was, and we felt the wakes of several boats as they passed close enough to save the waypoint and come back for their own shot at whatever might lie below the surface.

I tried to ignore them as we planned the next dive. Mac wanted to identify the ship, Ray was intent on further exploration of the hold, and I had to find some kind of clue to justify this endeavor. By now, Martinez likely knew where I was. He might not know who I was with or that we had taken Gross's boat, but underestimating his abilities had gotten me in trouble before.

With our dive plan set and the tanks topped off,

we relaxed on deck to kill the remainder of the surface interval. Planned correctly and with the assistance of the on-board compressor, we could do four dives before the buildup of nitrogen in our bloodstreams started to affect the bottom times. Anything less than twenty minutes was not worth the effort.

I continued to scan images on my phone, hoping for an easy identification. A search for Civil War-era wrecks yielded more vessels than I could count. It seemed that the Gulf had seen most of the official action, with New Orleans and Galveston being key cities in the war. The vastness of the Atlantic made it harder to patrol and the Navy, based in Key West, the lone Union outpost in the area, patrolled the waters as best they could.

The east coast had less of an official history, but the Bahamas, lying fifty miles to our east, had been a hotbed for smugglers. And smuggling meant wealth. My guess was that the ship below us was either a confederate blockade runner or a union patrol. In either event, there was the very real chance that there was wealth aboard. If Gross had been interested, it was likely not of the perishable variety.

"Time to gear up," Mac called out.

I checked my computer and noticed we had about ten minutes until we could start the next dive. Mac was not one to sit and wait, however, and we were just about ready to hit the water when the last minute expired.

The current had noticeably decreased and we dropped easily to the bottom. Without the energy it had taken to reach the anchor on the first dive, I hoped my air consumption would improve. We reached the site of the main wreck at about the same time and each went our separate ways. Ray soon disappeared in the metal frame and Mac finned around the stern, hoping to find something to identify the wreck.

I hovered above the smokestack, wondering

where to start my search. Trying to imagine Gross's last dive, I had originally surmised that he'd heard a boat directly above and shot to the surface. And in fact, every so often I could hear the vibration of a boat somewhere above. Underwater, sound travels well, except identifying its source or direction was impossible. Looking up to the surface would have been the only way that Gross could have known there was a boat above.

I glanced up and saw the hull of the *Reale* bouncing on the small waves at the surface. At this depth, provided the visibility was good, he could have easily seen another boat. His actions in the few minutes after he'd seen it were what had gotten him killed. It was out of character for an experienced diver, especially when it would take only another minute to safely reach the surface, to bolt and risk his life, and though his tank had been empty, I found it unlikely he'd been out of air.

I saw Mac's bubble trail moving along one of the

masts and decided to follow. After reaching him, we looked at each other, exchanged the okay signal and I dropped back. As an experienced salvor, he might see things that I would pass by. He stopped several times to brush the sand off a fitting or part, but continued on. Because she was mostly buried in the sand, there was nothing I saw that could identify her; hopefully Mac's more experienced eye would spot something.

Just as we had rounded the bow, I heard an engine above. Trying to imagine what Gross had gone through in the last moments of his life, I looked up. The only thing visible was the disturbed water from the hull of Gross's boat popping in and out of the water as the waves lifted and then dropped it. The engine noise grew louder, though, and I continued to look up. A minute later, I saw the shape of a hull coast to a stop next to the *Reale*. The propellor stopped and the frequency of the engine noise lowered, indicating it was in neutral.

I felt the breath tighten in my chest when I

realized the hull had the same profile as my center console. I glanced down at my dive computer; we were only thirty minutes into our planned fifty-minute dive. I doubted Mac or Ray would be happy, but feeling like Gross must have, I had to surface.

Removing the brass clip from my BC, I banged it several times on my tank to get Ray's and Mac's attention. It took several repetitions before they acknowledged me and I pointed up at the surface. Ray shook his head, immediately recognizing the profile of the hull; he had the same boat as well. Mac had a different kind of concern in his eyes; one of having our find discovered.

We headed for the surface, careful to not exceed the speed of our bubbles. Mac held a hand out flat when we were about ten feet below the hull, signaling us to hold there. We adjusted the air in our BCs to obtain neutral buoyancy and waited. Mac motioned to the far side of Gross's boat and, maintaining his depth, headed in that direction. Ray and I followed.

He was counting on using the hull as a blind spot where, unless the newcomer was peering directly over the gunwale, we would be hidden. Reaching the side, we popped our heads above the surface.

The only sound I could hear was the purring of the small outboard aboard the center console. We were under the bow flare of Gross's boat but unable to see anything, and I motioned toward the stern. It appeared we had been unobserved up to this point, and though it would have been easier to inflate our BCs we left them in their partially inflated state and finned toward the dive platform.

Once I rounded the corner of the boat, I saw the forest green T-top of the center console, which confirmed my guess as to the identity of our visitor.

Mad now, I removed my fins and placed them on the platform, then climbed out of the water, spitting out my regulator as I stepped onto the deck. I didn't have to search. Just inside the wheelhouse, Susan McLeash stood with her hands on her hips, staring at me.

"What are you doing here?" I asked as I pulled the mask off my face and tossed it to the deck. I was about to drop my tank when I saw another figure emerge. He came slowly and when I saw the limp I knew who it was. He propped his boot-encased leg on the larger boat's gunwale before shifting his weight across and standing on the deck.

"You've gone off the rails this time, Hunter." Her phone emerged from her pocket and she took several pictures.

"You trying to cut me out? Just like Gross," Slipstream spurted.

I thought for a second before deciding, that if I wrote a memoir, this would be called *The Case of the Odd Couples*—first Maria and DeWitt and now these two. I was surprised this couple had reunited after the scene at the restaurant last night, but I also knew how shrewd they both could be. Susan's instincts were as finely honed to be in the wrong place at the right time as Martinez's were for the podium. There was no doubt that in his drug- and alcohol-induced state Slipstream, in an attempt to impress her, had regaled Susan with stories of treasure.

"You want to explain what you're doing here? The boss is pissed and wants you back at headquarters now. Using a crime scene like this."

It sounded like a scolding from a kindergarten teacher. Despite her superiority complex, she knew she crossed the line more than I did and needed to watch her step. There had been several of her transgressions, mostly involving firearms, where I had covered for her. "I could ask you the same question," I told her.

She hesitated and I watched her eyes as they moved past me to the dive platform. "And who is this?"

I wanted to leave Mac's name out of it. He was here doing me a favor and I knew his distaste for publicity. Living with Mel, his girlfriend, on a remote island in the Keys, I knew he craved privacy. Turning, I could see him cringe and I looked back at Susan. It wasn't her that he was looking at.

"Mac freaking Travis," Slipstream spat around his cigar butt. "Now this is getting interesting."

Chapter 22

Mac ignored the introduction and climbed over the transom. Ray followed. Both men ignored Susan. Mac removed his mask, leaned over the gunwale, and cleared his nose before stepping right into Slipstream's personal space.

"Figures you had something to do with this." He walked past the startled mate, sat on the bench, and removed his dive gear.

"What is he doing here?" I asked Susan. while looking at Slipstream.

"It seems I have to use my own sources to get the truth."

It sounded like we now had an Internal Affairs department at the Park Service headed by none other than Susan McLeash.

"Y'all stop bickering," Ray said, pulling a beer out of a cooler he had brought. He offered one to Mac, who shook his head and grabbed a bottle of water. "We're out here working the park. That's the job, isn't it?"

"I have a claim to whatever's down there," Slipstream said. "Gross and me, we been dragging magnetometers around here for years."

I wondered how this was going to go if there was value to a wreck that lay inside the park boundaries. If DeWitt had issued a permit to salvage it, he had done so without authority, but from his constant request for the coordinates where Gross was killed, he apparently hadn't. "This is federal property. There are no claims here."

Mac suddenly perked up. I looked in his direction, but he held his tongue. I knew him well enough to know he wasn't going to say anything, and that was fine because both Susan and Slipstream were here for their own personal gain. Suddenly we were at a standoff.

"Go on back," I told Susan. "We'll finish up here and I'll go see Martinez."

She suddenly looked unsure of herself. If her goal had been to catch me red-handed at something out of line, she had failed. Her meaningless reprimand was all she had accomplished. While I waited for her to make up her mind, I realized Slipstream was missing. It didn't take long to find him.

Stepping out of the wheelhouse, he held the coral-crusted munition that Ray had recovered. "Just like Gross said."

He rotated the object in his hands, almost dropping it twice. I knew at one point it had had enough firepower to take out this ship. Mac must have thought the same and grabbed it from him.

"Y'all don't know what you're sitting on," Slipstream said. "Or what Gross was really up to."

"Maybe you could enlighten us."

By revealing that he knew something about the wreck, he now had all of us, including Susan, staring at him. I needed to stop his true confession. He must have told her something to get her out here, but it was obvious from the look on her face that she didn't know everything. If Susan figured out what we were sitting on it would be on the internet within hours—and Martinez would be making an appearance on the evening news. Leaning to my side, I released the bungee strap on the tank next to me and pushed it forward enough to unseat it. Thirty pounds of steel rolling around the deck of a rolling boat is enough to stop anything and as we scrambled for the tank, I pulled Mac aside and told him to take Slipstream below and sort him out.

Mac nodded and while Ray and I chased down and secured the tank, the two men disappeared. While we worked, Susan sat in one of the deck chairs with her feet curled up under her, likely more concerned about her recent pedicure than what was happening around her.

I couldn't hear the conversation, but could tell the difference in Slipstream's demeanor when he emerged on deck. There was going to be no dramatic reveal. With him contained, I had to get rid of Susan. In the company of four men, however, that was going to be a hard task. I had learned over time that the easiest way to remove her from the equation was to make her a better offer.

"Think you can track down Jim DeWitt, the state inspector? There's supposed to be some huge extravaganza this afternoon at the Savoy. Maybe you could get an invitation and check it out." I could see from the look on her face when she heard the words *Savoy* and *extravaganza* in the same sentence that she was already mentally browsing her closet for what to wear. A look of indecision crossed her brow when she found nothing appropriate—but there would be shopping and that settled it for her.

"Good idea. I'm tired of running around with

deckhands anyway." She took one more look around and carefully climbed over the gunwale to her boat.

"Deckhand... I'm a goddamned partner," Slipstream muttered.

He was as relieved as we were to see her go. I could see it on his face. He was where he wanted to be now, where he felt at home, and where he had a chance to take some riches from the waters that, as of yet, had withheld any reward. Mel Fisher's famous creed, *Today's the day* echoed through my mind when I looked at the newfound optimism in Slipstream's expression. The famous treasure hunter had said those words thirty years ago when his crew had found the motherload of the *Atocha*.

Mac was clearly not happy with him aboard, but as we watched Susan head back to headquarters, I think he was relieved that at least one of them was gone.

"Where did they find that piece of work?" Mac asked, watching her leave.

Her boat was porpoising through the waves, barely on plane. I found myself rooting for her by association, willing her to adjust the trim. Finally, she dropped speed and the boat leveled out, but it was far from an efficient attitude. I wondered if Mac's opinion of the Park Service dropped a notch until I remembered that when I had first met him I was as much of a novice boater as she appeared.

"Might as well get wet again before she does any damage," Ray said.

We agreed and Slipstream was given a stern warning to stay away from the electronics. I doubted, with him having the run of the boat for almost an hour, that he could, and volunteered to skip the dive and babysit. It had already become apparent that whatever had killed Gross had occurred above the surface of the water. As much as I would have liked to dive, topside was where I needed to be. Besides, a little quality time with my "partner" was probably a good idea.

Ray and Mac hit the water, both taking large mesh bags to collect any artifacts that might help identify the wreck. That left me staring across the deck of the boat at Slipstream.

"Got any more of those pills, I might tell you a story."

I'd had enough of being his private pharmacy. "I don't have them. They're back in the truck." It was at least the truth.

"You have no idea how freaking irritating this thing is." He reached down and released the velcro straps holding the boot in place. It fell free and he moved his leg around like there was nothing wrong with it. There was no guilt at all when he stood up and started walking normally around the deck to restore the circulation. There was no apology for his deception when he tossed it overboard and sat in one of the deck chairs.

"Seen a beer floating around."

I didn't want to hand out Ray's stash, but I

would offer one to get him to talk. "Maybe you tell me what you know first."

He rolled the cigar in his mouth. "There was a whole lot of action out here both before and during the Civil War that ain't recorded in the usual places. See, lot of rich southerners wanted to be hedging their bets and moved their wealth out of the states, you know—just in case."

"I heard the Union set up blockades."

"Damned Bahamas got about a thousand islands and they was more interested in New Orleans and the Gulf Coast. Besides, them islands"—he chewed on his cigar and looked to the east—"they been a pirate and smugglers' haven since old Chris Columbus landed there. Ain't no way of blockading them."

The cigar almost disappeared into his mouth. "Soon as word got out about what was being run across the Stream, them pirates sprung up again, only they called them privateers then."

He paused for effect and I started imagining the wreck below us loaded with gold and silver.

"It was complicated times and probably not like you're thinking. You see it was the privateers, with the blessing of the Confederacy, that were after the treasures. Willing to split the recovered goods with the government for their sanction, the privateers raided any boat they saw on these waters in an attempt to enrich themselves and keep the South's money in the South.

"And unlike the Spanish, who were fanatics about record keeping, there are no records of what went on here." It had been pirates robbing smugglers—neither wanting to attract attention. There would be no records of whatever was below us. I checked my watch. Ray and Mac had been down for thirty minutes already. I had another twenty minutes to finish my interrogation.

"You worked with Gross on finding this?"

"Towed a goddamned magnetometer around for

weeks. You'd be surprised how much crap is out here. Dive after dive of crap."

I'd learned quite a bit about artificial reefs; the nicer term for *crap*. The dumping of debris was better regulated now, but in the past, mountains of tires and other environmentally dangerous objects had been dumped on the ocean floor. "And what about hunting down the Spanish galleons?" That was how Gross had made a name for himself.

"Goddamned Ponzi scheme. You think you can go out and raise money, telling backers you're looking for steel ships with no manifests or records? These are one percenters handing over money mostly for bragging rights and the romance of it all. They ain't interested in steel ships. You want to see how this works. go check out Bugarra's party later."

"So, he found these wrecks and paid out some of the undocumented finds to his investors?"

"Right on, special agent."

I wondered what a state archeologist's interest in

steel ships was. "And DeWitt?"

"Goddamned state wants a piece of everything more than fifty years old. Hell they'd want a piece of me if I was down there." He laughed.

Just as he said it, I heard a boat coming toward us. Unlike when we'd been underwater, I could easily tell its direction and turned my head to the northwest. A large center console was up on plane, heading right toward us. For a minute I thought it was the Miami-Dade Contender and readied myself for a confrontation. As it approached I saw outriggers flopping from the bright red T-top and realized it was a private boat.

I didn't have to wait long to see who it was, and wasn't really surprised when a few minutes later I could see Jim DeWitt at the helm. He continued directly toward us, ignoring the two dive flags flapping above us. I yelled across that there were divers in the water, but his wake had already reached us and he idled alongside.

"What the hell are you doing? We have divers in the water."

He ignored the comment. "I could ask the same question. You have a permit for salvaging this wreck?"

I was pretty sure I had the upper hand. He was a state inspector on federal property. I decided to call his bluff. "You're within the Biscayne National Park boundary. The state has no jurisdiction here."

That shut him down for a minute and I watched as his face grew red. He knew I was right; now I needed to figure out what his true interest in this was.

Chapter 23

What I really needed was a maritime attorney; the closest thing I had was Martinez. Despite Susan's visit, I thought I might have his support in this. A Gill Gross wreck resting inside the park boundaries was big, even if it wasn't a Spanish galleon. It would probably mean another TV interview—one that I would be sure to miss.

"Because we're a branch of the federal government, one phone call is going to set a dozen attorneys to work on this." If it came down to a pissing battle between the feds and the state, the feds usually won, if by no other means than out-resourcing the locals.

"I am asking in the name of archeology to preserve this site until we can sort this out," DeWitt said.

I had no intention of marking or exploiting it and was speaking for myself when I agreed. Unless of course the site affected my murder investigation, which somehow kept finding itself on the back burner. Mac and Ray could be trusted. Neither wanted the kind of trouble that involved bureaucrats or lawyers. Slipstream would have to be watched, but that was standard procedure now, anyway.

"If that's all?" I asked the state man before releasing the lines and pushing his boat off.

"You haven't heard the last of this, Hunter."

He said this as he was moving away. Mac and Ray appeared by the dive ladder as if they had been waiting for him to leave. I could smell the cigar in Slipstream's mouth behind me.

"Guy's a freaking prick." The cigar smell moved closer.

There was no question that we agreed on that. There was something about the smug look on

DeWitt's face as he'd pulled away that told me I wasn't done with him. There were more than a few contradictions about the man, starting with how he could afford the boat he had just pulled up in on a state archeologist's salary. Working for the state, I didn't think he could be making much more than I did. The twin-engine thirty-footer cost more than I made over several years. His relationship with Maria Gross was also troubling. There certainly appeared to be more going on between them than just paperwork.

What I needed now was some time; I had to get DeWitt off my back. Susan had to be neutralized as well, and I figured that the best way to do that was to go directly into the belly of the beast—back to headquarters.

"You guys want to do another dive or have you seen enough?" It was close to one already and they would need over an hour's surface interval in order to get any kind of bottom time for a third dive.

"I got enough," Mac said. "We want to see anything else, we're gonna need to run the blowers." He looked around at the dozen or so boats on the horizon. "We do that now, it'll put up a cloud of sand; that'll be like chum to yellowtail. Best done before daylight."

"Yeah, spear gun, too. Some big snapper around that stack," Ray said.

"Great. Let's head back in and sort out what we've got."

"What about me?" Slipstream asked.

I had purposefully ignored asking his opinion. "I'll take you back to your place." For the first time today he took the cigar from his mouth.

"Y'all are just writing me off." He puffed out his chest and tossed the cigar overboard. "You think I'm old and washed up, just scrounging scraps. Let me tell you something." He patted his pockets and removed a fresh cigar. Taking his time, he unwrapped it, bit off the end, and placed it in his mouth. After rolling it around a few times, he continued. "Been at this game since y'all were in diapers. And that's you, too, Travis. I worked with Wood before you came along, and then some after. You're not the only one the old boy taught."

I was lost now. I knew Wood was Mac's girlfriend Mel's father, and it was he who had bought and originally lived on the island out by the Content Keys. He was also famous for building or repairing half of the fifty odd miles of bridges in the Keys.

"You were nothing but a drunk then and it looks like nothing's changed," Mac said.

Slipstream backed away; he chewed hard on the cigar and spit out a chunk. I knew he was going to get defensive and this whole conversation was already sideways. It was bad enough having to untangle Justine and Grace. I didn't need to referee a fight between Mac and the old mate.

"You'll be here when we dive again," I promised him.

That seemed to appease him. Ray went forward to secure the anchor after the windlass did its work. I made it back into the wheelhouse and we started toward headquarters. Once we were underway, Mac motioned me toward the back deck.

With the twin diesels running and the water slapping against the hull, we had to yell to be heard, but I was confident Slipstream, who was watching us carefully with a butt-hurt look on his face, couldn't hear.

"You better watch that guy. Him and Wood had a partnership for a while. Guy's a snake. Never caught him red-handed, but we thought he sold some of the artifacts off a wreck of the 1733 fleet before they split it."

"Doesn't surprise me." I told Mac about the waypoints on his computer. "He's a slippery one, but better to keep an eye on him than let him run loose."

"We'll disagree on that." Mac looked at the water ahead of us. "I'd like to get this a little more organized and come back. I can bring some equipment and if we get out before sunrise, fifteen minutes with those blowers ought to open her up."

His interest almost sidetracked my priorities. "I have to get a legal opinion first."

"Yeah, probably for the best. Back in the day, we'd do the work and let'm know later. Nowadays it's not worth even looking, though that Federal angle you got is worth looking into."

The ornamental lighthouse on Boca Chita Key passed on the port side. Ray had taken the direct route back to headquarters and now, inside the protection of the barrier islands, the two-foot waves dropped to a light chop and the engines purred as the deep V cut easily through the water.

Mac took advantage of the quiet. "This whole thing has gotten all upside-down. If it weren't for private money, no one would be out looking for wrecks. There's a bit of history for sure, but thinking it's safe on the bottom of the ocean is a fallacy.

Especially down here in the tropics. You've got worms and the shifting sands and storms break up and cover whatever's left of even the best-preserved wrecks. If it don't come up, it's going to get lost forever."

I had heard him rant about bureaucrats before and knew that it had to be special for him to work a salvage job anymore. His interest in Gross and this wreck proved that. Living out on the island, he had few bills and worked his traps far enough out that FWC left him alone. It was a simple life for a not-so-simple guy.

"Being inside the park changes the rules."

He nodded and continued to watch the water ahead. After several minutes of silence, I left him to his thoughts. While we continued in, I started to rehearse what I was going to tell Martinez. There was little point in hiding anything from him and thanks to Slipstream, he knew the general location. The irony that the wreck lay just inside an imaginary boundary negotiated by the same bureaucrats we were cursing wasn't lost on me. The park boundaries were arbitrary, especially on the northern and eastern edges. Stiltsville had been included in the eighties, expanding the northern end to form a parallelogram; the wreck lay within its outside angle.

I was ready with my speech, but it was going to have to wait. When we pulled into the common channel leading to Bayfront Park and the small headquarters marina, Ray cut the wheel and worked both throttles to make the tight turn. Once we were inside, I saw the commotion on the docks—Susan wasn't the only one who'd found out what we were up to. The media had as well.

I saw Martinez standing uneasily on the floating dock. Though this kind of attention was usually what he lived for, he seemed like a fish out of water, outdoors in the actual park, and not behind a lectern. I could see the distressed look on his face when the cameras turned away from him and instead focused on Gross's boat. If the turning basin in the marina had been several feet wider, I think Ray would have goosed the throttles, using the thrust from one engine in forward and the other in reverse, to spin the boat and escape. But it was too late. The only way out was to back out and, with the blind corner and narrow channel, that was a sketchy endeavor. I felt the rpms rise in the engines under my feet and for a moment thought he was going to go for it anyway.

I made it to the wheelhouse before he could commit and reassured him that it was safer to run toward the bullets than away from them. Dealing with the media, as my experience a few days ago clearly showed, was not my forte, but I did understand that these guys were like heat-seeking missiles. Once they found a target they were relentless—and unforgiving.

Ray backed the forty-foot boat into one of the open slips. The one Johnny Wells used for the ICE Interceptor would have been perfect, but the quad-powered boat was there. We barely fit between the pilings of the slip and the bow jutted out into the channel.

Martinez marched toward us with the cameras and reporters on his trail. I'd seen his boat skills and hoped he knew better than to try and help us with the lines in front of the cameras. Mac ended up saving him from that fate. He hopped over the gunwale after swinging two lines with bowline knots over the outside pilings. In seconds, we had the boat secure.

I lost sight of Mac in the throng of reporters, who were now thrusting microphones toward Martinez. He still looked confused and I saw his eyes move toward the boat. Needing answers to hold their attention but also a minute's reprieve to debrief me, he eyed the boat. I knew he was well out of his comfort zone and nodded to him. Making my way to the point along the port side where the dock was closest to the boat, I kicked a stool toward the gunwale. Fear was in his eyes as he stepped gingerly onto the boat and, seeing the stool, took a quick step down.

"What the hell, Hunter?"

I'd thought helping him aboard might have gained me some points, but that was not the case. He turned back to the crowd on the dock and raised a single finger, asking their indulgence while he stepped into the wheelhouse with me.

"Who was that guy?"

"What guy?" I had heard the sound of Jesse's Beast starting from across the channel just after Martinez boarded. Mac would be out of the parking lot by now. I knew if I wanted to preserve our friendship that he would have to stay anonymous.

"Never mind. Give me something." He glanced back nervously at the press, who were milling around and taking pictures of Gross's boat while they waited.

"Found the wreck Gross was diving on when he was killed."

He looked at me, not sure how this was going to play.

"It's ours. Just inside the boundary by Stiltsville."

Relief spread across his face and he actually slapped me on the back before stepping out of the wheelhouse. The reporters flooded to him, but now he was in his element. His decision to make the announcement and hold his little press conference from the deck of the boat was as much stagecraft as his fear of crossing back to the dock.

Ten minutes later the dock was deserted. A smile remained on his face, but I could see the calculating look in his eye, like he was an addict looking for his next fix. He was craving more media attention and relying on me to get it for him.

"You have a plan?"

Chapter 24

I'd just shown him an ace, but I knew I had better keep the rest of my hand close. Martinez's usual routine after an appearance was to find where his golf buddies would be for happy hour and make sure the TV was set to the correct news channel. With the find of the wreck, his interest in the murder would quickly fade. I knew I wouldn't have much more time until he was looking to me to either solve the case or abandon it. I had a feeling the fundraiser was going to be my last shot at finding the killer.

Checking my phone, I found a message from Justine that said she was heading to work early and to let me know what time we were going to the fundraiser. There was nothing from Susan, not that I'd expected a report. I had enough confidence in my assessments of her personality to know that if there was a party with money being thrown around, she would figure out a way to get in. The problem right now was getting myself there—and what to do about Slipstream.

He had proven resourceful, persistent, and even a little creative. I didn't have enough pills left to knock him out and after the request for gas money from the lottery babe, I knew that locking him in his apartment wasn't necessarily going to keep him there. Then I had an idea from the Tao—and decided to use the force instead of oppose it. "You going to that party at the Savoy?" I asked.

"Bugarra can throw a party. Hot women and free booze. Bunch of high-rollers ain't about to hand me a dime, but I'm not above scrounging for pennies," he said bitterly.

He looked down and let the cigar droop from his lips. I didn't have to be an expert in reading body language to figure out how he felt. But he would be there and that was what I wanted. The fundraiser was my one shot to see everyone associated with Gross in one place. Backers, competitors, and hangers-on would all be there, but without a disruptor, it could turn out to be an innocuous affair. Looking at the broken man sitting on the gunwale, I thought I might have my answer. He knew the players, and between his gruff manners and years in the business, he wouldn't be shy about letting people know he knew where the bodies were buried.

"Come on. Let's get you something to wear." He perked up immediately. I checked my watch. It was already pushing two and I looked down at my outfit. Boardshorts and a stained long-sleeved fishing shirt were not going to cut it for me, either. There was no time to run back to Adams Key or to stop at Justine's. JC Penney's would have to do for both of us.

An hour later my wallet was lighter, another expense that I wasn't likely to get reimbursed for unless I shot the equivalent of a hole-in-one at the event. Leaving the store, we looked more like Twinkies than I would have liked. Both of us wore button down, Hawaiian-style shirts and flat-front shorts. Dress flip-flops replaced our worn boat shoes. If I could do something about the cigar in Slipstream's mouth, he might pass as presentable.

I texted Justine and told her we would be by in half an hour. She immediately sniffed out the *we* and called me. It took almost the entire ride to the crime lab to explain why taking Slipstream was a good idea and even after that she still wasn't convinced, but I wasn't expecting good behavior. What I wanted from him was to elicit the responses that showed the real people beneath the façades. I'd seen him do it before and he was quite good at it.

The map app on my phone accurately estimated our arrival time and when I pulled into the parking lot of the lab, Justine was waiting. I wanted a quick face-to-face with her. "Wait here. I have to smooth things over with the boss." I got out and heard him through the window.

"Ain't that always the truth. Nice lady you got, though."

Justine came out of the building before I'd reached the entrance.

"Nice," she said, pecking me on the cheek.

At least she approved of my clothing selections. Taking a look at her, I was glad I'd made the attempt. I smiled, wondering how I had gotten so lucky.

"You need to do something about his cigar."

That was her only comment as we approached the truck. Slipstream relocated himself to the backseat and Justine brushed off the passenger seat before setting her bag on the floor and sliding in.

She took a second to evaluate her escorts before buckling her seat belt. "You both look nice."

I knew there was a *but* coming.

"You going to lose that stump in your mouth?"

"You think I've never mixed with these people

before. Don't worry about me; I'll blend right in."

I both hoped and doubted that would be the case. On the way to the beach, I told Justine about finding the wreck and our dives. When I mentioned the visit by DeWitt she asked if I had talked to Grace since we had seen her at Gross's house.

"No, I guess she's wrapped up in Morehead's murder investigation." I had actually been so involved with finding Gross's treasure that I had forgotten about the dead attorney. Justine, working from within Miami-Dade, had a different perspective.

"Maybe you should call her."

That was unusual, coming from her. "Okay. What's up?"

I saw her glance in the backseat. "I don't know, but there's something going on here."

I was pretty sure it was because of Slipstream that she didn't say more. As much as I wanted to know right then, it would have to wait. Justine seemed preoccupied and Slipstream knew better than to say anything, making for a quiet ride to the Savoy.

It was like entering a different world when the traffic came to a halt about a hundred yards from the hotel entrance. From where we sat, we could see the line of expensive cars, with valets scurrying like rats to move the people to the party and the vehicles out of the way. I've used my Park Service truck and credentials to avoid these kind of situations before, but this time I sensed it was better to be invisible. To that effect, I pulled into the left lane and drove past the entrance.

"What are you doing?" Justine asked.

Slipstream leaned forward in the backseat.

"I want to go into this incognito, not be identified as the agent investigating Gross's death the minute they see the truck," I said. I had thought about taking her car, but with Slipstream chewing on the cigar behind me, I didn't think that would be a good idea. As it was, I would have to add a detailing of the truck to get rid of the smell onto my expense report.

Several other people, all driving ordinary vehicles, must have had the same idea as me. The parking lot for the hotel next door was full, as was the strip center across the street. Finally, about a quarter-mile from the Savoy, I found a spot and parked.

"What about my foot?" Slipstream whined as his limp suddenly returned.

Justine got out of the truck and grabbed her bag. Walking over to Slipstream she recoiled her leg as if she was about to nail him with a side kick to his ankle, and he stopped. "Now for the cigar." She pulled it out of his mouth and tossed it into a nearby trash can. A smile crossed her face for the first time since I had picked her up.

Slipstream grumbled something and started walking ahead of us. I purposefully hung back several paces to distance myself from him. It was time he earned his keep and that meant he had to go in alone.

I also wanted to talk to Justine.

"What's up with Grace?"

She looked down. "Okay, I guess it's pretty obvious we have a history."

I kept my mouth shut and let her continue.

"So, there was a case a few years ago, just when I started. Evidence went missing, some very expensive jewelry. I was assigned to the case and processed the pieces. Then they disappeared from the evidence locker.

"Internal affairs started an investigation. They found the surveillance tapes were missing and the evidence log had been doctored. It was a high-profile case and fingers were pointing everywhere."

"Did they ever figure it out?"

"No, the suspect went free. It was one of Grace's first cases as a detective and she ended up taking the fall." She paused and I could see a tear in her eye. "But I did my own investigation and discovered it was her old partner."

"Tracy? Did you tell her?"

She shook her head. "Believe it or not, there was another winner before him. I wanted to talk to her, but it would have been like telling someone their spouse is cheating on them. I took it to Internal Affairs. They questioned her and she turned on him."

"Why does she hold it against you?"

" I went on the forensic evidence; it was all I had."

She said it like she was making an apology. Her inquisitive nature was one of the things I loved and admired about her. "That's your job."

"I should have given the evidence to Grace instead of the IA people. I put her on the spot and she had to turn on her partner rather than having the opportunity to uncover his duplicity and expose it in her own way. The former action made her a rat; the latter option would have gotten her a commendation. She's never trusted me since."

Reputation meant everything to Justine and I

could guess how much the distrust had hurt her, as well as the never-ending water cooler talk amongst the detectives. When I had first met her, several had given her a hard time. I had thought at the time it was because she had rebuffed their advances, but now suspected it was more complicated.

That explained Grace's bad partner karma. It would take a long time for the memory of turning against a partner to fade—if it ever did. "But she blames you?"

She shrugged. Justine was a top-notch forensic tech, not a politician. I wondered now if the swing shift had been her idea after all, or if it had been a punishment. Inadvertently, in their attempt to punish her, they had put her where she excelled.

We entered the circular driveway to the hotel and our attention turned to the spectacle in front of us. I had heard that Boca Raton and Palm Beach were the places to be seen, but this looked like the red carpet at the Oscars. I grabbed her hand and squeezed, trying to reassure her that I was here for her.

Right after the valets, dressed as sailors for the event, opened car doors for the attendees, a handful of people in officers' uniforms discreetly checked them in with an iPad. The guests were then directed toward a carpeted entry, which placed them in front of a pair of photographers. After their photos were taken, they disappeared inside the lobby.

We had encountered our first hurdle and I was glad we had parked down the street. Now, my choice was to either use my credentials or we would need to walk back to the adjacent hotel in order to access the beach and walk over to the Savoy. I again chose discretion. I saw Slipstream moving away from the entrance as well. He had already made that decision.

After backtracking to the hotel next door, we entered without any questions and walked straight through the lobby to the beach access, where floor-to-ceiling glass revealed the Atlantic Ocean. Walking back outside, we passed two pools on our way to the beach. Once we hit sand, we took off our flip-flops and Justine slipped them into her bag. From where we stood we could hear the sound of reggae coming from a live band. Well-dressed people stood in groups, drinking what looked like rum punches from souvenir cups and swaying to the music.

Another group was down by the water. A large white tent obscured a good deal of the view, but I could clearly see the ribs of a Spanish galleon sticking above the waterline.

Chapter 25

*E*xtravaganza was the right word for the event. As we moved closer, I could see a group of notable charities had been given table space under a large tent by the bar. Their displays were professional and their booths well-manned and busy, but the main attraction was at the end, taking up almost a quarter of the tent. A half-dozen large-screen TVs that together made one large display showed a video of an underwater scene, with divers bringing load after load of gold, silver, and jewels up from the bottom.

Below the screens was a banner proclaiming *Shipwreck Hunters, Inc.*, the proud sponsor of the event, aptly called the Shipwreck Ball. A server passed by with a tray of what I guessed were rum punches in commemorative mugs. I grabbed two from the woman dressed as a wench and handed one to Justine. I didn't want to drink, but blending in was important.

Together we walked by the smaller tables being operated by the charities. They were doing a brisk business, but nothing compared to the crowd in front of the host's table. Sipping the fruity drink, I noticed the contact information for *Shipwreck Hunters* proudly etched into the plastic mug. If for some reason you missed their pitch, it would come home with you.

Walking up to their display I saw the excitement as men and women clad in bathing suits ran up to redeem what looked like commemorative coins. We stood there together, sipping the smooth and powerful drinks faster than I had wanted to, and watching the people come and go until I figured out what was happening.

After registering with one of the pirate-clad, iPad-holding employees, each guest surrendered a credit card that was quickly swiped on the device.

Then the patrons were directed to the large tent by the water that we had seen from the other hotel. This appeared to be a changing area, where the guests donned samples of several designer swimsuits. They were given masks, snorkels, fins, and a mesh bag. Once clothed and equipped, several employees helped them adjust the snorkeling gear and ushered them into the water by the shipwreck.

Some returned to shore faster than others, but all eventually came back with a bag full of what looked like coins and jewels. These were taken to the tent, counted, and recorded by another pirate with an iPad. The new treasure hunters were rewarded with a chit to use at the charity tables. The coins were then placed in a commemorative mesh bag, which I'm sure had the contact information for *Shipwreck Hunters* on it.

Even though the event was clearly staged, the participants were jubilant about their finds. With fresh drinks in hand, they quickly made the rounds of the charity tables and dispensed their chits.

It was brilliant. Everyone who participated came away with a dose of treasure fever, and though the host wasn't asking for anything now, with their contact information going home with everyone on the coins, bags, and plastic mugs, in a day or two their website would be flooded and their phones would be ringing off the hook with potential backers. This morning I had learned about Gross's scheme to lure investors, now I was witnessing a different but equally elaborate method. I could only wonder if these guys actually looked for treasure or if their real income came from encouraging backers to part with their cash.

One man stood out. He was larger both in stature and attitude. Dressed as a commodore or admiral, he worked the crowd, shaking hands and patting backs. There was no doubt he was the man behind *Shipwreck Hunters*—and I needed to talk to him.

Justine was, of course, one step ahead of me and steered me to a quiet corner of the tent. She held her phone between us and scrolled down the home page for *Shipwreck Hunters*. Yesterday when I had checked, the page had been all about the fundraiser. Now that everyone was already here, the landing page was an elaborate ad to lure in backers. At the bottom was a picture of the man himself: Vince Bugarra. A blurb below the headshot gave a short bio.

What I wanted to see was the expression on his face when he was confronted with questions about Gross's death. Justine slid her phone back into her bag and we started to work our way across the room. Before we reached Bugarra, I spotted Susan McLeash, complete with her new outfit, walking toward the tent with DeWitt's hand at her elbow. She carried a mug and took a deep sip before leaning closer to him. At least she was playing her part. I steered Justine away from them. Just as we were out of their path, I saw Maria Gross make a beeline toward Bugarra. I grabbed Justine's hand and pulled her back, wanting to see what this was all about.

A line of reporters and cameras followed Maria as she approached Bugarra. Surrounded by fawning fans—mostly women—he was oblivious to her approach. Maria marched toward him with what could only be described as attitude. With her head held high, she looked like she was on a mission. The crowd noticed and closed in on the scene. Fearing the worst and wishing I had my weapon, I moved closer as well.

When they were ten feet apart, Maria broke the spell and called out Bugarra's name. It wasn't said maliciously or as a threat; it sounded quite the opposite. Seconds later, the crowd had parted and I was temporarily blinded by a dozen camera flashes as nearby reporters took pictures of what looked to be a happy couple.

With his large arm draped around her shoulders, he pulled her into an embrace and they kissed. Some guests applauded; others looked on with questions on their faces, but the scene had served its purpose—every eye in the room was on the couple.

Maria broke the spell again. After another kiss for the cameras, she led the crowd to the changing tent. As if she was the Pied Piper, they followed the first lady of treasure hunting down the beach and waited outside while she changed. A few minutes later she emerged in a designer suit that must have been waiting for her. With her snorkeling gear and mesh bag in hand, she walked toward the water.

Several waiting photographers followed her as she walked waist-deep into the surf, adjusted her mask, placed the snorkel in her mouth, and entered the water. Behind me I felt the press of people, some watching the water and others trying to get in and out of the tent in time to swim with her.

Her celebrity status surprised me. From her dress and attitude I had assumed she traveled in these circles, but these people were fawning over her.

Maybe it was because she was the daughter of the famed Gill Gross, or because of her apparent relationship with Bugarra, or the theme of the event, but here she was the queen.

Then I saw the joker. I had been so enthralled in the event I had forgotten about Slipstream. From the corner of my eye, I saw him enter the water from the beach of the hotel next door. There were security guards on the property line to keep the public away from the staged wreck, but a strong swimmer could easily enter farther down the beach and swim to the site.

Though his body looked like that of a much older man, I guessed that Slipstream had probably had thousands of hours in the water. He would easily be able to reach the site, and as I watched him stroke toward the exposed ribs of the wreck I failed to come up with one good reason for him to be there. If they'd been offering cash for the fake coins and jewelry the participants clutched in their mesh bags as they emerged from the water, it could have been that. But with Maria in the water, I suspected trouble.

Questions flashed through my mind as I grabbed Justine and led her to the changing tent.

"What are we doing?" she asked.

"Slipstream. He's in the water. We have to stop him."

She understood immediately. We skipped the changing part and went right to the pirates handing out the snorkeling gear. I wasn't sure if it was the distressed looks on our faces or the flash of my credentials—probably the former—but they reluctantly handed each of us a mask, snorkel, and fins. There was no time to change, so I pulled off my shirt and tossed it on the sand. Justine did the same and we entered the water with our gear in hand.

Because I had little beach-diving experience, I followed Justine's lead and waded out until we were waist-deep. We put our masks on and started breathing through our snorkels. Turning our backs to the water, we put on our fins and slowly backed in until we were submerged.

The visibility of the ten-feet of water surprised me. It was, better than I had expected, considering the surf and shallow water. As we swam seaward, the wreck became visible. The setting was so real I couldn't resist the urge to reach out and touch one of the beams. I knew they had to be fake, but they looked so real.

A quick tap revealed they were made of fiberglass. Whoever had staged this had done a masterful job. The ribs, partially sheathed with the same material, led down to a deck that was partly covered with sand. It looked so real that when I saw the glint of a plastic coin, I almost reached out for it.

Drawn in by the scene, I had nearly forgotten our purpose. I looked up and scanned the water for any sign of either Slipstream or Maria. I had seen pictures in Gross's house of Maria aboard the salvage vessels with dive gear on. Growing up with Gross for a father, she would likely be an accomplished diver. With both video and still cameras recording her every move, she would have gone to the deeper side of the wreck to show off her abilities—that was why she was here.

Justine, who was several feet ahead of me, looked back. Once we made eye contact, she pointed at something ahead. I finned hard toward the seaward side of the structure and saw a figure darting for the surface. The floral print bikini told me it was Maria. I looked around for Slipstream but, not seeing him, motioned to Justine for us to split up. I moved toward the bow and she went toward the stern.

With one eye on Maria and the other scanning the water for Slipstream, I watched as she took several breaths, jackknifed her body, and slid back beneath the water. It all looked effortless and the cameras were recording every movement as she kicked twice, reached the bottom, and scooped up a handful of coins.

Two divers with video equipment recorded her every move as she brought her bounty back to the surface. After several breaths she descended again. Her body movements were becoming more exaggerated as she tired. If Slipstream was going to make a move it would be soon. The entire surface was now covered with prone bodies watching Maria. There was no way to differentiate one from another.

All eyes were on her as she prepared for another dive. Several people were oblivious to the show and still diving on their own. Some were close enough that I could see them clearly, but those on the far side of the wreck were just blurs as they kicked toward the bottom.

My eyes were drawn back to the surface when, without warning, Maria tucked her body into a pike position, preparing for another dive. With one knee against her chest and her other leg fully extended, she slid below the surface. Below her a burst of bubbles caught my attention and I started to breathe deeply. I had seen regulators in free flow, but this was different. Looking for the source, I saw two pairs of fins spinning together behind a section of the wreck. A cloud of sand quickly rose from the bottom and obscured the fracas.

I took one last breath and descended. Maria's entries were designed to conserve air; mine used half of my supply. By the time I reached the bottom, I was already struggling and had to pull myself from rib to rib just to hold myself under. I felt the first convulsions before I reached the bubbles and knew I was in trouble. Fortunately Justine had seen the fight as well and was finning toward me. She gave me a thumbs-up and continued toward the two men.

I struggled to reach the surface. It was shallow enough that there was no risk of an embolism, but I knew I could drown in knee-deep water if I passed out. Whether I made the decision consciously or not, I bolted for the surface, spit out my snorkel, and started gasping for breath. With a fresh supply of oxygen, I dropped below again. This time I was right above them and dove straight for the bottom.

Below me, Maria was scooping up coins when suddenly a hand reached out and grabbed her ankle. There was no doubt who had hold of her.

Chapter 26

Slipstream had timed his grab well, waiting until Maria had expended her air supply. The other diver he'd fought with was in the process of rescuing his buddy, whom Slipstream had knocked unconscious when he had taken his tank. With the amount of silt kicked up from the fight, there was little visible evidence that anything was wrong from the surface.

There was surprisingly little fight left in her before Maria's body went limp. Shallow water blackout is a real concern of even experienced free divers. In seconds, with her brain no longer communicating with her muscles, her mouth would open and she would drown. It would look to the world as if she had gotten stuck amongst the wreckage while trying to extract a piece of treasure.

To everyone but me and Justine, that is. I was on the surface, gulping air in huge breaths. Deep down I knew that was only going to introduce more carbon dioxide than oxygen into my system and it took several seconds, ones that could mean her life, before I was able to slow my breath rate and inhale some useful air. After several breaths, I tried to mimic Maria's entry and slid below the surface.

The struggle had reduced the visibility of their location—the only indication was the cloud of silt. It wasn't until I entered into it that I could identify the people, and that was really only by the color of their fins and swimwear.

Slipstream had a stranglehold on Maria, who lay limp in his arms. Justine struggled to tear his arms away, but I could tell she needed to surface. Like a tag team in a wrestling match, I tapped her shoulder and took over. She bolted for the surface.

Free divers know how to slow their heartbeats and use the smallest motions possible to conserve their air and extend their bottom time, but I wasn't near that class and was surprised by how quickly my supply was gone. Too soon after I had taken over for Justine, I felt the first convulsion in my diaphragm and knew I had only seconds before I too would have to surface.

Deciding Maria was going to die unless I did something drastic, I stopped pulling on Slipstream's arms and tried to grasp the regulator from his mouth. Instead of trying to free her I hoped that if I crippled him he would release her. The change in tactics surprised him, but just before the rubber came free of his mouth I could feel his teeth bite hard into the molded mouthpiece. He tried to shake me off and I was just about to release my grip to renew my air supply when my arm tangled in one of the other hoses.

A standard regulator setup has four hoses attached to the first stage, which is fixed to the tank. One is the main regulator hose, slung to the right of the diver. On the diver's left are the low-pressure inflator hose that is connected to the buoyancy compensator and the high-pressure hose that goes to the gauges. The remaining hose is an alternate air supply called an octopus. It was that hose that I became tangled in, and my struggle released the regulator attached to the hose from its clip on the vest.

Grabbing for the floating mouthpiece, I stuffed it in my mouth and took two large breaths. The playing field had been leveled. Slipstream turned his attention to me and I saw Justine grab Maria's body and take it to the surface. That second of relief cost me and suddenly the lights went out.

I had no idea how long it had been or how I had gotten there, but I knew I was on the surface. I heard voices around me before I saw anything. Slowly, I took stock. My head was fuzzy and there was an intense pounding behind my ear. I tried to open one eye.

"He's awake," I heard someone say.

Suddenly there was a flurry of activity around me. I opened my other eye and it took a second for the world to come into focus. With all of the faces above me, I thought I might be seeing double, but when I saw there was just one Justine, I started to sort things out. She leaned over and brushed my hair out of my eyes while several other people worked around me. I was conscious enough to hear them call out my vital signs, which were in the stable range.

I started to sit up, but felt arms wrap around me. Giving in, I lay back and let them fuss with my head while I tried to remember what had happened. I recalled fighting with Slipstream and then Justine swimming Maria to the surface. That was it, and soon I thought I felt well enough to have the blanks filled in.

"Maria?" I asked.

"She's fine. They just airlifted her to Jackson Memorial. You saved her life," Justine said.

"What about Slipstream?"

"No sign of him. There were several boats in the vicinity, or he could have swum down the beach."

"Can I sit up and have some water?" I realized how dry my mouth was.

"Take it slow," she said.

"Forget that. He's all right. We gotta get that bastard."

I knew that voice, and it didn't make me happy.

"Cool it. We'll get the guy, but let's take care of the living first."

This time it was Grace's voice. She came to my other side and with Justine's help eased me against the combing of the Miami-Dade Contender. Grace handed me a bottle of water while Justine got directly in front of me and stared into my eyes. It wasn't a weepy kind of romantic moment, but a concussion protocol. From the look on her face, I knew I had failed.

"You've got a bad head wound, probably needs

some stitches. Definitely a concussion." Justine summarized my injuries.

"Good then," I said, taking a long drink of water and trying to stand. Between the waves rolling the boat and the confusion in my head, I wavered. Pushing away Justine's help, I grabbed one of the rod holders behind the seat and pulled myself to a standing position. The roll of the boat caused me to stumble and I looked around. The tide had started to ebb, causing the sloppy conditions. We were just beyond the soup, the breaking waves and white water closest to the beach.

Worried more about the cameras on the beach getting pictures of him rescuing the treasure heiress, the Miami-Dade captain had ignored basic seamanship and the boat was being slowly pulled toward the staged wreck. He was focused only on the beach and didn't notice that as we were being drawn closer the waves had spun the boat parallel to shore and were breaking high against the port side.

Using the stainless steel pipe that held the t-top, I pulled myself to the helm. "You see a thirty-foot, narrow-beamed boat out there? Red top with outriggers?"

"That's half the boats in Miami," he said dismissively.

"We find that boat and you'll have your arrest." That got his attention and he either figured enough pictures had been taken or there'd be more coming if he added the arrest to his resumé. Without reading the breaking waves, he quickly spun the bow toward the open water. The timing couldn't have been worse and a wave broke across the bow, flooding the boat. Instead of matching the seas, he hammered through them and we smashed into several more waves before we hit water deep enough that the waves rolled under the hull. Much to the delight of the captain, I leaned over the side and threw up. Wobbly, I made my way back to the helm. Water streamed through the scuppers as he accelerated and we were quickly running on plane, but without a destination. "Radar work?"

"Yeah." He called one of his men over and instructed him to search for a boat with a thirty-foot signature.

I wished we were aboard Johnny Wells's Interceptor instead of on the police boat. Between the power of his electronics and his skill, Wells could zero in on birds working bait from five miles away. Watching the Miami-Dade officer fumble with the controls, I realized the effort was futile. I wasn't sure how long I had been out, either, but guessing from the position of the sun over the beach, it had been at least a half hour. DeWitt's boat could be twenty miles away by now.

If there wasn't going to be a chase, I wanted off the boat. The question was where. The receding tide had made a beach drop too dangerous and we were several miles from Government Cut and about the same from Haulover Inlet to the north. To complicate matters, I had no idea which way they had gone—assuming my theory was correct.

Slipstream would be going down for at least the attempted murder of Maria Gross, which led me to believe he had killed her father as well. He would have had to overcome the effects of drugs and alcohol to meet Morehead in Coral Gables the night before we found him, but watching him toss off the walking cast like he was suddenly healed had revealed to me his deviousness. I was starting to feel stupid when Grace moved to the helm beside the captain and took my place. She made the decision for me and the boat spun to the south.

Minutes later, we entered Government Cut. The captain ignored the maximum speed warning and blazed through the channel. Finally, he cut the wheel hard to starboard and rounded the point. Without our losing momentum, our wake hit the Miami Beach Marina; within seconds millions of dollars' worth of boats were banging against the floating docks and each other. He seemed oblivious as he cut the wheel again and coasted to a stop at the fuel dock.

Grace hopped off first and deciding this was our stop, Justine and I followed. Before my foot hit the dock, he had already started to spin the boat back to the cut. Between the moving boat and the change in height to the dock, I lost my balance and dropped to my knees. Grace and Justine immediately surrounded me, but I brushed them off and slowly rose. Concussion or not, I had to keep going.

I needed to find Susan and see if DeWitt had left the party. Justine and I had jumped in with most of our clothes on and I realized my phone was still in my pocket. Pulling it out, I pressed the power button, expecting a blank screen in response, but surprisingly it lit up. The manufacturer's claims that it was waterproof were correct.

Susan's number was near the top of my text history and I quickly pecked out a few questions for her. Seconds later the phone dinged and I saw her response: an emoji that I couldn't see. It could have been smiling or crying, for all I knew. I texted back a string of question marks and asked her to call me.

There was a longer pause this time. I answered immediately and could tell by the background noise that she was still at the Savoy. "What's going on over there?"

"Helluva party—thanks, Kurt." She hiccuped after saying my name.

This was when Susan was at her most dangerous. Asking her to do anything could and probably would be misconstrued. As an officer of the law, I should have alerted hotel security, but I just said I'd get with her later. All I could gather from the brief conversation was that the incident hadn't put a damper on the party. For all the people watching from the beach and hotel knew, what had happened to Maria could easily have been part of the program. "Where's DeWitt?"

"Kurt, I met this guy. He's a calls himself

commodore ..."

I pulled the phone away from my ear in disgust. "She's drunk. We're on our own," I said, looking back and forth between Justine and Grace. The last thing I needed was the two of them to start fighting.

My phone rang again. This time I knew the number and answered right away.

"I think we should dive that wreck again," Mac said.

He sounded excited—for Mac. "What'd you find out?"

"Tomorrow morning. Same place and time okay?"

I answered in the affirmative and realized he had disconnected before I could say good-bye. Justine and Grace stared at me. "That was Mac. He wants to dive the wreck again tomorrow."

"Sounds pretty secretive," Grace said.

"That's just the way he is." A thought crept into my mind, but if things hadn't been so jumbled in there I would have seen the answer to our problems right away.

"I'd like to tag along," Grace said.

"You're not going without me," Justine added.

I almost said it was okay if they played nice, but just before the words came out of my mouth, my brain processed my thoughts.

"We don't have to find Slipstream and DeWitt. They'll come to us."

Chapter 27

Justine was not going to be left behind and I knew better than to fight with her. Besides, I would have been wrong in excluding her because I wanted to protect her. She was as competent as I was, even more so underwater, and that was where we were going.

Grace called for a cruiser to pick her up and offered us a ride back to my truck. Justine shrugged and we accepted.

"Where's your partner?" I asked.

"Water and boats aren't his thing," she said.

I knew there was more, but vowed to stay as close to both as I could to avoid him. While we waited, I worked through my plan. Mac wanted to dive the wreck. Though he wouldn't say what it was over the phone, obviously he had discovered something. Justine and I would go with him. Grace had offered the use of the Miami-Dade Contender. They could take up station a few miles away and keep a radar surveillance of the site. I thought it might be better, and less alarming to DeWitt and Slipstream, if Johnny Wells and his ICE team would help. First of all they were unknown, and second, DeWitt, at least, would know that Miami-Dade was out of their jurisdiction in the park. ICE as a federal agency wouldn't be questioned.

I called Johnny and left a message.

The police cruiser pulled up and we jumped in. By now the surge of adrenaline was long gone and I was feeling tired and had a headache. Justine, sitting next to me in the back, yawned. I grasped her hand and we sat in silence as we were driven back to the beach. Johnny hadn't called back yet and I had to agree to let Grace handle the surveillance. I hoped my concussion wasn't affecting my decision-making process. Knowing she was going to be involved was reassuring, but the crew would be forever suspect in my mind.

We agreed on a time. There was no update from Susan—not that I'd expected a report—and no reply from Johnny Wells, either. Turning south on the Turnpike, I cringed when I saw the flashing yellow warning signs indicating road construction ahead. We had passed the golden hour. Between seven and nine, post rush-hour, and pre construction, were usually the only times you could run a speed limit sortie from Miami to Homestead.

Brake lights illuminated the road ahead, and I saw the four lanes start to merge to three and then to two. It was almost an hour later before we reached our exit. Thankfully the Homestead-Miami Speedway was dark or we would have had another delay. It only took a few minutes to drive the empty surface streets to the park entrance.

The gate was locked and I tried to blame my fumbled attempt with the key on the low light, but I had to admit the head injury was affecting me. After opening the entrance we drove in and parked behind the headquarters building. I turned the power off on my work phone and stuck it in my pocket, then locked the truck. Justine started toward the sidewalk that led around the building to the dock, but I grabbed her hand and pulled her in the other direction. Staying to the shadows, we walked the perimeter of the parking lot. Through the gaps in the mangrove-lined shore it was hard not to look at the offered views of the open bay with Miami's skyline in the distance, especially when my brain was creating halos around the lights. It always struck me as some kind of weird irony that the hundred and fifty thousand acres of pristine water was this close to Miami.

There was no dodging the cameras pointed at the dock, but we did our best to use the boats for cover. Passing Susan's and my matching center consoles, we snuck toward Gross's boat. Martinez would know it was gone when he got here in the morning and with no way of locating me, suspect that I had taken it. In a backward way that was exactly what I needed. I would have liked for the mission to be off the books, especially because Mac was involved, but felt like this was my window of opportunity. If I wanted to draw the killer into my trap, I had to let Martinez know where we were. But it had to appear to be a mistake.

I hoped my plan would work because by now, I had confused myself. After stepping aboard in what I hoped was a blind spot, I fired up the engines while Justine untied the lines. Before we made the turn to the main channel, I looked over at the empty slip where the ICE Interceptor docked. The forty-foot quad-powered cruiser was equipped for multi-day missions and it looked like Miami-Dade was my only option now. A few minutes later, we were chugging out of the channel toward the moonlit barrier islands.

Once clear of the channel, I handed the wheel to

Justine and grabbed my phone. Meeting Mac back at the headquarters dock, or even at Bayfront Park, was too close to home and Martinez's network for me to be comfortable. I left a message to meet at Alabama Jack's on the south end of the bay. Not only would we avoid the office, the location was closer for him and an easy run to the wreck site. After disconnecting with him, I texted Grace that we would need her team.

There was no point trying to talk over the engines. We had been through a lot tonight, but it was not the first time. Both of us knew this was going to end tomorrow; there would be time to process everything later. Justine expertly slid the boat to the dock and just as I dropped the fenders and jumped up with the bow line, I heard Zero barking and the screen door to Ray's house slam behind him. I wasn't sure if he had some kind of radar that told him Justine was here, or whether it was the unfamiliar boat that had drawn him, but seconds later, and panting heavily, he skidded to a stop on the concrete dock. My reactions were either slowed, or he was moving too fast, but we ended up in a pile on the dock

"That you, Hunter?" Ray called from his deck.

"Yeah, sorry about that." I brushed myself off, got up, and slid the line over the cleat.

I silently cursed when I heard the wooden steps creak under his weight as he came down to talk. He would want to know what was going on and I was tired and in no mood to relive tonight's adventure. Instead, I told him about our plan to dive with Mac in the morning. He readily accepted the invitation that had not been really offered. Wondering whether I should tell him no, I decided against it. There was plenty of room aboard and another able body might be of value. In addition, my wobbly legs made me worry about my ability to do anything. "We'll be leaving at six to get Mac."

"Good deal. I liked that dude."

I smiled at the compliment. A reference from Ray was about as good as it got. After securing the boat, we said good night and started toward the house. Zero followed and I looked back for Ray, who had disappeared. With no one to call him off, I guessed we had a guest for the night.

My head was banging and ringing and I wanted to go to bed, but there was one more thing I had to do. Sitting at the bar, I opened my computer and typed out a quick message to Martinez. I knew how to push his buttons and embedded several lines about Miami-Dade handling things that were sure to get a reaction from him.

The bait was in the trap; now I had to hope the dominos fell like I had planned.

Several months ago, I would have been in a tired but wired state, but I dropped off as soon as my head hit the pillow. Justine waking me up every hour to check on me only reminded me that I wasn't getting used to the stress of my job, but had been hurt worse than I wanted to admit.

The alarm went off and I looked over as Justine opened her eyes and smiled. I felt a tingly feeling that I knew, unless I got out of bed right now, would only delay us. As it was, I heard a knock on the door. Apparently Ray was from the *on time is ten minutes early* school.

I sat up and got both feet on the ground with no ill effects from the head injury, starting toward the door with Zero behind me. He bolted out when I opened it. With toenails clicking down the stairs, he made a beeline across the freshly cut lawn to his food bowl. He at least had his priorities in line.

"Y'all comin'?"

"Be right down. What's the weather?" I asked.

"Another beautiful day in paradise. Now we better scoot before the boss gets up. He's not going to be happy about this."

I knew the pressure was on to make an arrest and if my plan worked, we would. "Okay, go fire her up. We're almost ready."

I could envision him shaking his head as he walked down the stairs. We had apparently not met whatever his criteria was for being ready. I wasn't too worried about Ray's opinion, but knew we better get moving. Justine walked toward me with a small cooler hung from her shoulder. She leaned in and kissed me. We paused for a minute, enjoying the contact, but I broke it off. I could almost hear Ray tapping his foot on the dock.

A few minutes later, we slipped the lines and let the current move the boat from the dock. The tide was pushing in Caesar Creek, and Ray pressed down on the throttles once we were in the middle of the channel. With the offshore breeze that usually came with the dawn here opposing the current, small whitecaps had formed in the cut. He spun the wheel, deciding to take the inside route. Now, with the current behind us, he started to accelerate. After belching a small cloud of smoke the engines started to purr. Ray pushed them harder and we came as close to plane as the heavy boat could maintain.

Mac was waiting on the back dock of Alabama Jack's when we pulled up. Without a word, he grunted and slung his dive bag over the gunwale and followed it onto the deck. I introduced him to Justine, which got one side of his mouth to curl up. He went directly to the helm and talked to Ray for a minute before coming back to the cockpit.

Ray had no interest in our conversation and pushed the throttles to their stops. The sun was just below the horizon now and the low clouds and red sky told us some weather was coming. I could see Mac's lips move as he tried to talk and inched closer. It was futile, and as Ray cut through Old Rhode's Bank and headed to the outside of the barrier islands the noise increased, as did the boat speed.

We sat, each in our own heads, for the forty minutes it took the boat to cover the fifteen-odd miles to the wreck site. When Ray finally dropped speed, my ears rung from the noise and my body vibrated, but I was wide awake now. Slowly as my hearing returned, so did my headache. Mac went back to the wheelhouse, spoke to Ray, and came back to the cockpit with a large buoy.

"Toss it," Ray called out from the wheelhouse. "Kurt, go up and get the anchor ready."

Mac dropped the buoy over as I went forward. The line, with a four-pound dive weight attached to its end, unwound. It went slack, and with the aid of the current, slowly paid out the rest of the line. With the wreck marked and the buoy telling Ray the state of the current, it was only a minute before he had moved upwind and called for me to drop the anchor.

I felt it grab and tied the line off to the bow cleat to take the pressure off the windlass. When the boat swung, I looked back and saw the buoy fifty feet behind us. Slowly, I released the line, careful to keep a wrap around the cleat and let the line slide through my hand until Mac snagged the buoy with a gaff.

After securing the line, I went back to the cockpit where Ray, Justine, and Mac were waiting for me.

My phone rang and all eyes turned to me. Mac was wary; Ray and Justine worried that Martinez had found us. I hadn't had a chance to enter any of my contacts besides Allie and Justine, but when I looked at the display, I recognized the number as Grace Herrera's.

She and the Miami-Dade Contender were in position outside the Boca Chita harbor. They had a clear radar signature on the *Reale* and there were no other vessels within the five-mile ring. We were alone for now. It was time to set the trap. But before I made that call, it was time to find out why we were here.

Chapter 28

My plan was for Susan McLeash to be the patsy and trigger the chain of events I needed to bring the killer to us. I could always trust her to do the wrong thing, especially if she thought she was going to benefit from it. The strong possibility that she had a hangover from the potent drinks served at the fundraiser last night should keep her reasoning skills low enough that she wouldn't question me. I just had to get Martinez to send her. Coming from me, an order or even a request for help was going to be suspect.

Taking a deep breath, I pulled my work phone out and turned it on. I could almost see the invisible beacon broadcasting my location to the mothership. I fully expected Martinez to be in a near-panic state by now after reading my email report of the incident last night and seeing the pictures of the Miami-Dade Contender getting credit for Maria Gross's rescue all over the news. I was pretty sure one of the first things he did every morning was to locate me anyway; the report would just push his buttons. After a few minutes, I turned the phone back off in an attempt to make it seem as if I was purposefully trying to deceive him, but for some reason I'd had to use it.

I felt the boat vibrate and turned to the transom. While I had been setting my trap, Mac and Ray had lowered the mailboxes and now, with the engines running, the prop wash was being redirected to the bottom. Seconds later a sand cloud started to form. If my location didn't get Martinez to act, the reports he was surely going to get about the silt cloud would. Over the next few minutes it turned from a cloud to a storm. The wind and current were in our favor and took the silt toward the mainland. Just to make sure it was brought to his attention, I texted Grace from my personal phone that it was heading toward her and asked her to anonymously call the Coast Guard.

After about fifteen minutes, Ray shut down the engines. "What'd you figure out?" I asked Mac. He had estimated it would take about thirty minutes before the visibility would return. Now was as good a time as any to hear what he had found.

"She's a Civil War-era ship. Belonged to the Confederacy. I'm betting it's the *Sumter* we have down there. Launched in 1859 as a raider, she was commanded by Raphael Semmes. He penetrated the blockade around New Orleans, so I would suspect at that point the ship would be heavily loaded and worth taking to risk those odds. We know she made it through because she took out a slew of Union ships on her way around Key West."

"Do you know what she was carrying?" I asked.

"Interesting times back then. There were no manifests or sailing instructions recorded. They sank a whole lot of boats in that war, and when brothers are fighting brothers there tends to be some embellishment. Even the records available tend to be more fiction than fact."

"Okay, so how does that help us?" Knowing what was below us was interesting but not a game changer. Apparently, I was the only one who hadn't figured it out.

Mac went to his duffle bag and pulled out several papers. "This here's the layout of the ship. If there were to be anything down there ..." he stopped as if worried about being overheard if he said the words. Instead he pointed to two spots on the drawing. "I'll check this area, why don't you two have a look over here." He made sure that Ray and Justine understood and replaced the drawing in his bag, looked into the water, and started to gear up. "I'd say about fifteen minutes and we're good."

Justine and Ray followed his direction and soon the deck was cluttered with dive gear. While they prepared for the dive, I looked over the side. The water had cleared. Hopefully the mailboxes had moved enough material for the divers to recover something. That would only be a bonus. I moved my gaze to the horizon, scanning for the familiar red T-top I expected to see at any moment.

Checking my watch, I saw it was almost nine. Mac, Ray, and Justine were about ready to dive and I gave them the thumbs-up. I wanted to be going with them, but the head injury grounded me. Now, as I watched them check each other's gear and walk through the transom door to the dive platform, I hoped the concussion was not going to affect my ability to handle what I hoped was heading our way on the surface.

Justine turned and gave me a worried look. I gave her another thumbs-up and watched her take a giant stride off the platform, following Mac and Ray into the water. I was alone now and started to pace the deck, staring toward Miami where I expected to see the profile of DeWitt's boat appear at any minute.

After a half-hour, I started second-guessing myself. Maybe the plan was too complicated. I had worked it all out in my head, but anticipating the reactions of three people, even if they are known entities, was not exactly hard science. I also had to hope that the party had not taken anyone out of commission. Martinez would surely take the bait. By now, he knew I was out here and that there was something wrong. With my phone off, he would have no choice but to send Susan out to check on me. If her brain wasn't still saturated with alcohol from the party, she'd be shrewd enough to figure out what we were doing out here.

Confronting us alone wasn't her style. She would want backup, and after seeing her and DeWitt together last night, I was planning on her calling him to do her dirty work. Anyone that was anti-Kurt Hunter would be her friend, and I was sure the state archeologist had bent her ear about me.

The minutes ticked by and I was starting to

worry that Mac, Ray, and Justine would surface. For my plan to work, I needed them to be under. I thought about using the underwater horn on the boat to call them up, have them do a quick surface interval and go back down, but just as I was about to push the button, I heard my personal phone ring.

"Got them inside the five-mile ring. Looks like the boat you described," Grace said.

I quickly calculated their speed. The twin-engine boat would be running close to forty knots in these conditions. That would put their ETA inside ten minutes. As if on cue, I looked toward the west and saw a boat heading directly toward us. "I have a visual. You ready?" I asked Grace. She confirmed and I disconnected. With my pistol in hand, I went to the helm and pushed the button for the underwater horn. This was the agreed-upon signal and would give the divers a heads-up of what was happening. I then ducked down into the dark cabin to wait.

Within minutes, I heard the sound of the twin

engines approach and then drop. The bow wake pushed under and lifted the larger boat. I quickly hit send on my pre-written text: *Contact*.

I could feel the boat shift as someone moved on the deck. Sliding into the head, I closed the door and locked it. There would be no reason for whoever was on deck to suspect someone aboard and if they did happen to check the door, it was not uncommon for latches to jam on older boats. Less than a minute later, I heard the engines stop.

The boat settled and I relaxed. My watch said that five minutes had elapsed and I slowly unlocked the door and cracked it a few inches. I had only a partial view of the deck from here, but I knew I would have to be patient. Looking out the small hatch, I saw the bubble streams of the divers as they rose to the surface.

My heart was beating hard enough that I felt it in my ears as I waited. Fighting a wave of nausea, I stood ready by the door. Then I heard a loud noise that sounded like something was being dragged across the deck. Slowly, I opened the door another few inches to see what was going on.

Slipstream and DeWitt were clearing the deck. I didn't understand their purpose until I saw them reach for the access handles and slowly raise the hatch that exposed the twin engines. Slipstream then climbed down into the space and I wondered what they were up to. There were easier ways to disable the boat. When I heard the gurgling of water coming through the open seacocks, I knew I had misjudged them.

The clock in my head started ticking faster now that the boat was sinking. I wasn't sure how long it would take, but I could already feel it listing toward the port side. Slipstream climbed out of the engine room with a smug look on his face and they dropped the cover back and scattered the gear on the deck.

Bubbles breaking the water moved my attention to the stern. I couldn't see what was happening through the transom, but I could see Slipstream pull a gun from his waistband and point it at the water. I moved quickly, hoping to reach him before he fired, but just as I burst through the door of the head, DeWitt inadvertently crossed in front of the companionway and together we fell to the deck.

My head hit something and I felt the warmth of blood as my wound reopened. It took a second to clear my mind—a second too long. Slipstream, figuring I was now the bigger threat, had turned and pointed his gun at me.

"You meddling prick," he said.

"We gotta go. The boat's sinking," DeWitt got to his feet, grabbed my pistol from the deck, and moved to the gunwale adjacent to his boat.

Before he could reach it, I heard another boat coming toward us. "Drop it. Another murder isn't going to get you any richer." I heard myself say. It was as if it came from another person and made little sense, but I needed to buy some time.

"Hurry up, it's the police," DeWitt called to him and climbed onto his boat.

Slipstream looked around and fired several shots at the water. I hoped the divers, especially Justine, had descended to a safe depth to wait this out, but knowing all three of them, I wondered if the plan was still the plan. With his back turned, I looked around for a weapon.

Slipstream turned back to me, but just before he could pull the trigger the Miami-Dade Contender slammed into the port side. We were both thrown off balance and rifles were quickly leveled at Slipstream who dropped his weapon. Seconds later, two of the crewmen jumped over the gunwale and had him prone on the deck.

While they were occupied, I heard the engines on DeWitt's boat fire up. He had hoped to use the distraction to make his escape. I was back on my feet now and my heart leapt into my throat when I saw Justine clinging to the dive ladder on his boat.

Before DeWitt accelerated he turned toward us and paused. I found myself looking down the barrel of my own gun. I quickly ducked behind a fiberglass support for the flybridge, taking myself out of his sights. Mac and Ray were still in the water, and he hadn't seen Justine. That left only Grace and the captain aboard the Contender as targets. The captain was busy working the throttles and wheel, trying to keep the boat stationary. Grace lowered her weapon when she saw the barrel of his gun pointed at her and instead of dropping it, she ducked and jumped onto DeWitt's boat.

I could see the look in DeWitt's eyes. He was cornered and he knew it. There would be no escape unless he finished their plan to sink the *Reale* and kill the divers. Now there were a few more bodies to add, but he still seemed to think he had the advantage.

The muscles in his arm tensed and I felt helpless. I called out to him to no avail and hoped for a rogue wave to throw off his aim when I saw his finger twitch. I thought it was over for Grace, but it was Justine who, still hanging from the dive ladder in the instant before he pulled the trigger, jumped onto the deck. In one fluid movement she swung the air hose from her regulator around DeWitt's neck. She pulled him off his feet and the gun flew into the air. A second later, all eyes turned as it dropped into the water.

Chapter 29

The crew of the Contender worked with surprising efficiency. They hauled Slipstream over the gunwales and quickly had both him and DeWitt secured.

Mac and Ray had immediately assessed the situation and after climbing aboard were quickly in the engine room repairing whatever had been done to allow the boat to take on water. Slipstream had taken the sabotage one step further than I'd thought in his attempt to scuttle the *Reale* and keep the site of the *Sumter* a secret. Mac and Ray, having stemmed the incoming water, were now working on rewiring the pumps. Her engines would need an overhaul, but Mac and Ray had saved the boat.

I could barely hear Grace reading Slipstream and DeWitt their Miranda rights as the pumps finally started to remove the water from the *Reale.*

I was another story. After moving me to the Contender, Grace and Justine both fussed over my head wound in an attempt to stop the bleeding.

"Y'all need to get him to the hospital." Ray rose from the engine compartment and called to the captain of the police boat. "Me and Mac got this. Just send a tow."

I tried to get up and thank them, but Justine held me down. I looked up at her and Grace, working together to help me, and noticed something had changed between them. It would probably never be said out loud, but I sensed that a new bond had been forged—I could only hope so.

The captain started the engines and Justine rose and moved toward him. "Can you hold on for a second?"

I strained to see what she was up to as she climbed back aboard the *Reale.* Grace relaxed her grip on me enough for her to see as well, but not enough to let me stand. Justine went for her bag and pulled out a small dry box. She reached down into the hold and handed it to Mac. They exchanged a few words and she was back aboard the Contender.

"What was that about?" I asked her over the whine of the Contender's twin engines.

"It came from Gross's office. Some files he was working on. Figured Mac might be the one to figure them out."

I was coherent enough to know she had broken the chain of evidence. "You going to get in trouble for that?" I asked, glancing at Grace at the same time to see if things really had changed, and saw the two women exchange a conspiratorial look.

"Let's call him an expert witness," Grace said.

I tried to smile, but it hurt. Before I could thank her, the captain swung the bow of the boat toward Miami. The momentum of the boat caused me to fall back into Justine's arms. Not that I had any fight left in me, but if there was anyplace I wanted to be, it was right there.

About the Author

Always looking for a new location or adventure to write about, Steven Becker can usually be found on or near the water. He splits his time between Tampa and the Florida Keys - paddling, sailing, diving, fishing or exploring.

Find out more by visiting

www.stevenbeckerauthor.com

or contact me directly at

booksbybecker@gmail.com

Get my starter library First Bite for Free when you sign up for my newsletter

http://eepurl.com/-obDj

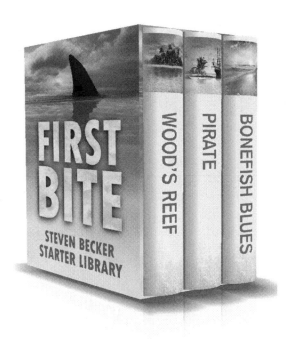

First Bite contains the first book in each of Steven Becker's series:

- **Wood's Reef**
- **Pirate**
- **Bonefish Blues**

By joining you will receive one or two emails a month about what I'm doing and special offers.

Your contact information and privacy are important to me. I will not spam or share your email with anyone.

Wood's Reef

"A riveting tale of intrigue and terrorism, Key West characters in their full glory! Fast paced and continually changing direction Mr Becker has me hooked on his skillful and adventurous tales from the Conch Republic!"

Pirate

"A gripping tale of pirate adventure off the coast of 19th Century Florida!"

Bonefish Blues

"I just couldn't put this book down. A great plot filled with action. Steven Becker brings each character to life, allowing the reader to become immersed in the plot."

Get them now (http://eepurl.com/-obDj)

Also By Steven Becker

Kurt Hunter Mysteries

Backwater Bay

Backwater Channel

Backwater Cove

Backwater Key

Backwater Pass

Backwater Tide

Mac Travis Adventures

Wood's Relic

Wood's Reef

Wood's Wall

Wood's Wreck

Wood's Harbor

Wood's Reach

Wood's Revenge

Wood's Betrayal

Tides of Fortune

Pirate

The Wreck of the Ten Sail

Haitian Gold

Will Service Adventure Thrillers

Bonefish Blues

Tuna Tango

Dorado Duet

Storm Series

Storm Rising

Storm Force

Made in the USA
Middletown, DE
26 September 2022

11231580R00234